The Day the Circus came to Stickleback Hollow

The Mysteries of Stickleback Hollow

By C.S. Woolley

A Mightier Than the Sword UK Publication

©2017

The Day the Circus came to Stickleback Hollow

The Mysteries of Stickleback Hollow

By C. S. Woolley

A Mightier Than the Sword UK Publication

Paperback Edition

For

Mills

Author's Note

Thanks for taking the time to read *The Day the Circus came to Stickleback Hollow*, I hope you enjoy it, there is much more to come in the series if you do! This particular book is set between Christmas and New Year so you'll have to wait for Christmas in Stickleback Hollow or 12 Days of Christmas in Stickleback Hollow to find out what happens on Christmas Day in Grangeback Manor.

The Characters

Lady Sarah Montgomery Baird Watson-Wentworth

The heroine

Brigadier General George Webb-Kneelingroach

Guardian of Lady Sarah and owner of Grangeback

Miss Grace Read

Lady Sarah's lady's maid

Bosworth

The butler

Mrs. Bosworth

The housekeeper

Cooky

The cook

Mr Alexander Hunter

A huntsman and groundskeeper of Grangeback

Pattinson

An Akita, Alexander's hunting dog

Constable Arwyn Evans

Policeman in Stickleback Hollow

Doctor Jack Hales

The doctor in Stickleback Hollow

Miss Angela Baker

The seamstress in Stickleback Hollow

Wilson

The innkeeper in Stickleback Hollow

Mrs Emma Wilson

Wife of Wilson and cook at the inn

Mr Henry Cartwright

Owner of Duffleton Hall

Stanley Baker

Son of Miss Baker

Lee Baker

Son of Miss Baker

Reverend Percy Butterfield

The vicar in Stickleback Hollow

Mr Richard Hales

Son of Doctor Hales

Mr Gordon Hales

Son of Doctor Hales

Lord Daniel Cooper

A gentleman from Tatton Park

Mr Stuart Moore

A gentleman of Cheshire

Mr Jake Walker

A gentleman of Cheshire

The Honourable Mr Wilbraham Egerton

Owner of Tatton Park

Mrs Elizabeth Egerton nee Sykes

Wife of Wilbraham

Mr Wilbraham Egerton

Son of Wilbraham & Elizabeth

Mr Thomas Egerton

Son of Wilbraham & Elizabeth

Mrs Charlotte Egerton nee Milner

Wife of Thomas

Mr Edward Christopher Egerton

Son of Wilbraham & Elizabeth

Miss Mary Pierrepont

Fiancée of Edward

Mr Harry Taylor

A gentleman in the employment of John Smith

Bairstow

Ringmaster and owner of Bairstow's circus

Mr James Christian

A retired missionary

Old Woakes

A retired soldier

Miss Gunn

A retired governess

Miss Beaumont

A governess

Mr Mitchell Claydon

An explorer

Miss Jessica Hales

Sister of Doctor Jack Hales

Miss Millie Roy

A charwoman

Miss Elizabeth Wessex

Fiancée of Mr. Harry Taylor

Mr Johnathen Mullaney

A gentleman of Cheshire

Mrs Abigail Mullaney

A lady of Cheshire

Mrs Ruth Cooper

Mother of Mr. Daniel Cooper

Mr Gregory Kitts

A gentleman of Cheshire

Mr Samuel Jones

A gentleman of Cheshire

Mr Luke Lumb

A gentleman of the Antipodes

Mr Timothy Wood

A gentleman of Cheshire

Mr Richard Ball

A gentleman of Cheshire

Mr Michael Hutton

A gentleman of Cheshire

Mr Joseph Blatherwick

A gentleman of Cheshire

Mr. S. Carter

The butcher

Mr Dominic Smith

A strongman

Miss Emily Read

Grace's sister, an acrobat

Mr. Peter Libby

A magician

Mr Toby Craggs

A clown

Mr Paul Curran

A knife performer

Mr Matthew Read

A lion tamer

Mr Michael Trott

An elephant handler

Lord Joshua St. Vincent

A young lord in the employ of Lady Carol-Ann

Mr Callum St. Vincent

A young gentleman in the employ of Lady Carol-Ann

John Smith

An Alias

Lady Carol-Ann Margaret de Mandeville, Duchess of Aumale and Montagu

The villain

Chapter 1

There is no greater simple pleasure in life than the joy of one's own company. At least this was true as far as Lady Sarah Montgomery Baird Watson-Wentworth was concerned. Growing up as an only child, she had quickly learned the value of being content enough with herself to spend hours on her own.

She was perfectly willing to be sociable when the occasion called for it, but she didn't have the need that others had of constantly being in the company of others, prattling away for fear that silence might descend.

Revelling in quiet time had not only brought Lady Sarah many hours of pleasure, but also a self-awareness that only comes from time spent in reflection on one's own character.

It had grown her into a woman of independence that was certainly not commonly found amongst the high society of London.

When she had come to live at Grangeback, as the ward

of Brigadier George Webb-Kneelingroach, being able to spend time in her own company had stood her in good stead, for though there were plenty of people living on the estate and in the nearby village of Stickleback Hollow, most of her time was spent in solitude. That is until the arrival of Grace.

Grace was her lady's maid and constant companion, and had been for a number of weeks. Christmas had passed, and both Sarah and Grace had been introduced to the traditions of the house.

It had been much easier for Grace to adapt to the celebrations than it had been for Sarah. Though they had celebrated Christmas in India, it was a very different affair to Christmas in Stickleback Hollow. But the festive period had given both Sarah and Grace chance to adjust to each other's presence.

Mr Alexander Hunter had also been spending a great deal more time at Grangeback since Sarah had been rescued from the asylum. This meant that Sarah now barely had two moments to herself during the day, and it was only when she went to bed that she was on her own and able to enjoy her own company.

It wasn't an unpleasant change in circumstances to be

faced with, but it was certainly different. On St. Stephen's Day Sarah and Alex both took part in the hunt along with members of the neighbourhood that included Mr Stuart Moore, Mr Jake Walker, Lord Daniel Cooper, Mr Richard Hales, Mr Gordon Hales, Mr Thomas Egerton and Mr Edward Egerton.

Sarah was the only woman riding with the hunt, though the ladies had all assembled along with the older gentlemen to lead the villagers as they followed the hunt.

The hunt began at Wilson's inn in the heart of Stickleback Hollow. The huntmaster was the Honourable Mr Wilbraham Egerton of Tatton Park, and it was his permission that riders needed in order to participate.

George had gone to talk to him on Sarah's behalf. Mr Hunter, as the best hunter in the county, was always permitted to ride as part of the hunt, but it was rare that he took advantage of his permanent place in the hunt.

News had quickly spread around the neighbourhood that Lord Daniel Cooper had proposed to Lady Sarah, but that his advances had been declined.

It had been something of a scandal in the neighbourhood, something that Sarah had not been subjected to before.

Most of the village had been relieved to hear that Lady Sarah had declined the advances of Lord Daniel Cooper. Since his arrival in the neighbourhood, he had not proven to be a popular figure.

There were certain things that the Lord of any manor was expected to do, and so far, Mr Daniel Cooper had failed to accomplish any of them. Country squires had judicial responsibilities as well as social ones, yet all that Lord Daniel Cooper seemed interested in doing was spending his days hunting and his nights hosting parties for the young men of the neighbourhood.

This had not gone down well amongst the villagers. Though Mr Henry Cartwright had been a poor businessman as far as finances were concerned, he had been very attentive to the needs of the people. This had led to many comparisons between the two gentlemen, especially as Mr Henry Cartwright still lived in the area and did a lot for the people.

On the morning of the St. Stephen's Day hunt, Grace awoke early and was surprised to find that Lady Sarah was already awake and dressed.

Sarah was waiting downstairs with George, surrounded by piles of boxes.

The household staff all assembled, and one by one, were given a box and then were free to do whatever they would with the rest of the day. Each box contained a number of gifts that the staff appreciated. Some contained exotic foods whilst others contained trinkets.

Grace was the last to receive her box and was surprised to discover that it contained a small silver locket. It was the most delicate thing that Grace had ever seen, and she was rendered speechless.

Once the festivities of the day had been taken care of, Sarah took her leave of the rest of the household and went to saddle Black Guy.

The destrier was waiting in his stable, already tacked when Sarah arrived. Mr Hunter was stood waiting in hunting pink with five brass buttons on the front of the coat. Sarah almost burst into laughter when she saw him.

"That is something I wasn't expecting," Sarah spluttered.

"If I am going to ride as part of the hunt, I have to look the part," Alex grumbled.

"Well though it does look strange to me, it does suit you," Sarah smiled.

"Then I will take that as some form of compliment," Alex replied with a raised eyebrow.

"We should go, otherwise we'll be late," Sarah smiled.

Though the men all rode red to hunt in, Sarah was dressed in a navy blue coat that Miss Baker had made for her.

The ride down to the village was a peaceful one. Thick snow covered the ground, and the lands around Grangeback were still.

Sarah breathed in the cold air and sighed. Though it had taken her a long time to adjust to the difference in temperature between India and England, she had found that she quite enjoyed the snowy winter.

Alex rode beside her, neither of them feeling the need to engage in pointless conversation. As they reached the edge of Stickleback Hollow, the sound and smell of the dogs drifted to greet them.

Around the inn, there were horses and riders all milling around in general excitement for the hunt to come. Mr Thomas Egerton was the first to spot Alex and Sarah as they arrived.

"Hunter! Lady Sarah!" he called with a broad grin on his face as he pushed through the throng to reach the pair. At the sound of Sarah's name being called out, Lord Daniel Cooper wheeled around and cast a dark look at the pair.

"Good morning, Thomas," Sarah replied with a smile as she gently reined Black Guy to a halt and dismounted.

"When my father told me you would be coming on the hunt, I couldn't quite believe it! What was even more unbelievable was that Hunter was going to ride with us as well. Father has been trying for years to convince him to ride with us regularly. Maybe now we'll get to see more of him," Thomas said warmly.

"No need to make such a fuss," Alex mumbled as he dismounted from Harald's back, "We need to go greet the Master," he said to Sarah. Thomas led the pair, and their horses, through the crowd to where the Honourable Mr Wilbraham Egerton was stood.

The pair greeted the Master, and Sarah listened as Wilbraham and Alex discussed the hunt, the dogs and who was to ride where from the hunt staff.

Sarah soon discovered that there were many rules and levels of etiquette that had to be observed during the hunt, and she was glad that Alex was there with her.

She was acutely aware of the number of hushed

conversations that seemed to increase as she found herself in the vicinity. It didn't occur to her that they were not only concerning her refusal of Daniel's proposal but her appearing with Mr Hunter as a companion as well.

After half an hour of waiting, the hunt had begun. It lasted for a few hours before the fox managed to evade the hounds. Once the Master was sure the fox was lost, they returned to Stickleback Hollow and Wilson's inn.

The drinks flowed and the number of conversations that centred in hushed voices around Sarah diminished. Many of them had been impressed by Sarah's riding ability on the hunt, and the desire to speculate on her social activities had soon lost its appeal.

As the afternoon became evening, Sarah and Alex made their goodbyes to the Master and the members of the hunt that had been talking with them. They rode back to Grangeback with the lamps lighting their way through the streets of Stickleback Hollow.

As they reached the edge of the village, the light of the stars was all they had to guide them, so they stuck to the roads instead of cutting across the fields.

By the time they reached Grangeback, Sarah was

falling asleep in the saddle. Alex sent her into the house and untacked their horses.

Sarah stumbled up the stairs and collapsed on her bed, still fully clothed.

Chapter 2

As the New Year approached, there was a change in the atmosphere of Grangeback and down in Stickleback Hollow.

The excitement of the hunt had passed, but it had replaced with a sense of desperate anticipation, and Constable Evans seemed to suddenly become exceptionally busy.

It wasn't until Sarah and Grace went down to the village on the day after the hunt that they discovered the source of the change in atmosphere.

The circus was coming to Stickleback Hollow. It was the first time that the circus had chosen to visit the village. In the past, there had been a few circus performers appearing at the fairs in Chester and Manchester, but now a real circus was coming.

Wilson's inn was a filled with people discussing rumours about the circus. The most popular myths included performers that could appear and disappear as though they were ghosts as well as people that could fly.

The posters in the village all said that the circus was going to be open on New Year's Day. A canvas tent, as well as a number of carriages and cages, had appeared in one of the fields close to the village, which belonged to Lord Cooper.

Lee and Stanley Baker both stood in Wilson's inn, and boldly told everyone that they had been up to the tent and seen everything.

They told tall tales about exotic animals and magical people that inhabited the circus. There were some who listened in rapture whilst others put the stories down to the wild imagination of the two boys.

Though most people from the village seemed to be sharing stories in the inn, Constable Evans was conspicuous by his absence.

Sarah and Grace left the comfortable atmosphere of the inn and walked to the police house. They knocked three times on the door, and a very grumpy looking Constable Evans yanked open the door.

"Oh, good afternoon, ladies," Arwyn said as he realised who it was.

"What's the matter?" Grace asked as Arwyn showed the two women into the sitting room of the police house.

"Nothing, just a few angry people in the village," Arwyn replied, shaking his head.

"What are people so angry about that it is affecting your mood?" Sarah asked as she sat down.

"There have been a number of items that have gone missing in the village; people are claiming they've been stolen. But with the exception of Miss Baker's leather tools, I can't find a shred of evidence that anything has been stolen," Constable Evans sighed.

"You think that people have just been extremely forgetful recently?" Grace frowned.

"With the festive season people have been drinking more, and it's well-known that many people forget what they have done during their inebriation. It wouldn't surprise me if these 'stolen' items were just dropped or given away whilst the complainants were drunk," Arwyn shrugged.

"Have you managed to find out anything about Miss Baker's tools?" Sarah asked.

"No, and strangely that seemed to be an isolated incident. There haven't been any other break-ins since," Constable Evans replied.

"Which is why you think that these other items haven't

been stolen," Sarah concluded.

"Nothing is appearing in any of the pawnshops that matches the items that have been taken. Aside from someone actually witnessing the theft of any items, there isn't much more I can do," Arwyn replied.

"What kind of things have been reported as being stolen?" Grace asked.

"A pocket knife, a fishing rod, Miss Baker's leather tools, a brass candlestick, a worn-out left boot, a silver fork, a pewter tankard and pearl broach," Arwyn listed the items with a sigh.

"So only the broach and leather tools are worth anything?" Grace asked.

"Worth is a little subjective; the fishing rod belongs to Old Woakes. To him, it was worth a lot, he can't really afford to replace it, and most of his food comes from fishing," Constable Evans shrugged.

"And all of these items have gone missing when?" Sarah tapped her chin thoughtfully.

"They've been reported as stolen in the last week," Arwyn confirmed.

"I see," Sarah screwed up her face in thought.

"There isn't a mystery to be solved here. There's nothing out of the ordinary, nothing that needs you to investigate," Constable Evans said in a tired voice.

"All of these people can't simply have become forgetful and misplaced these belongings. It just strikes me as strange," Sarah shrugged.

"Well then, feel free to talk to each one of them. I'm sure that you're going to come to the same conclusion I did," Arwyn sighed with resignation.

"Besides Miss Baker and Old Woakes, who else is missing property?" Sarah asked.

"Reverend Butterfield is missing the candlestick. The worn-out left boot belonged to Mr Christian – the one who lives at the cottage at the end of the lane. The silver fork was reported missing by Miss Gunn. The pewter tankard went missing from Wilson's inn. The pocket knife was Mr Claydon's and the pearl broach belonged to Miss Roy," Constable Evans replied.

"Thank you; we'll go and see them then," Sarah announced as she stood up.

"I still say you are wasting your time, but if your mind is made up, I know better than to try and stop you," Arwyn sighed and moved to stoke the fire.

"You're really convinced that all these items have been lost and haven't been stolen, aren't you?" Grace gave Constable Evans a slight smile.

"Who in Stickleback Hollow would rob their friends and neighbours?" Arwyn shrugged.

"Well, at one point you believed that Mr Hunter was capable of that," Sarah said pointedly.

"Yes, well, he's become a lot more sociable and much less gruff since then. Most of Stickleback trusts him now," Constable Evans shifted uncomfortably as he spoke.

"You thought Mr Hunter was a thief?" Grace asked in disbelief.

"He never really came into the village; he kept to himself, frightened children out of the woods and spent most of his time prowling around the grounds of the house. What else was I supposed to think?" Arwyn protested.

"Being anti-social doesn't necessarily mean someone is a criminal," Sarah frowned.

"Well I know that now, and I don't think Mr Hunter is the one stealing now." Constable Evans replied.

"Come, Grace; we'll leave Constable Evans to think on

his prejudices whilst we go talk to the villagers," Sarah swept from the room in a dramatic fashion. Grace followed close behind, trying her best not to giggle. Constable Evans was left to stand by the fire, feeling rather foolish.

"You don't really think that badly of Constable Evans, do you, my lady?" Grace asked as she and Sarah walked down the path of the police house.

"No, but it is always good to remind people of when their assumptions have led them into mistakes before, especially when they are doing it a second time," Sarah replied.

"But he just said that he isn't blaming Mr Hunter for the disappearance of all these items," Grace frowned.

"No, he isn't, but there is something strange about so many items going missing. It could be coincidence, but it is worth investigating and not dismissing," Sarah smiled.

"My lady, if I go too far, then please tell me, but are you sure that you are not looking for a mystery where none exists because you are bored?" Grace asked tentatively.

"Bored? I'm not bored," Sarah laughed.

"Since you recovered from your stay at the asylum, you have been rather restless, as though you were waiting for your next adventure. At this moment, you are more excited than I have seen you in weeks," Grace replied.

"Maybe I have been waiting for something to happen, and maybe there is nothing to these items being stolen, but you're wrong about me looking for mysteries. They come to me," Sarah grinned and marched in the direction of Old Woakes' cottage.

Chapter 3

Old Woakes' cottage was the closest building to the woods and the lake that ran around Stickleback Hollow. In his youth, he had been known as young Woakes, back when his father had been alive. He had served in the British Army under the command of the brigadier, and lost both of his sons to war.

His wife had died after the news of both sons perishing at the Battle of Waterloo had been received, leaving Old Woakes without any family to speak of.

He had taken to fishing to keep himself occupied during the hours when he wasn't at work. It was not something that most people would have considered a good hobby if they had been in Old Woakes' position, but it had suited him well enough.

The time alone gave him the chance to think and pray. He managed to let go of all the anger and pain he felt at losing the most important people in his life and became known as one of the most cheerful people in the village.

Fishing had become something that he did not only to relax, but in order to feed himself and provide an income when he could no longer work. George had given Old Woakes permission to fish in the lake and sell the fish that he wasn't going to eat.

Without the permission of the Lord of the Manor, Old Woakes would have been a poacher, something that would have landed him in trouble with Constable Evans, Mr Hunter and Brigadier Webb-Kneelingroach. He had also been granted a license when the Game Act was introduced.

When the fish were not in season, Mr Hunter took Old Woakes game from the estate upon George's instruction so that the old man wouldn't starve. All of this enabled Old Woakes to survive with a small income that provided him with the little necessities to get through daily life, but there was no way that he would be able to afford a new fishing rod.

As Sarah and Grace made their way down the street, they met a familiar face coming the other way with a face that was not so familiar.

"Ah, good afternoon, Lady Sarah, Miss Read. How are you both today?" Doctor Jack Hales greeted them in a sunny voice.

"Good afternoon, doctor, we're on our way to visit Old Woakes," Sarah replied.

"I see; may I introduce my sister, Miss Jessica Hales. She's come to visit me until after the New Year. Jessica, this is her Ladyship, Sarah Montgomery Baird Watson-Wentworth, and her companion, Miss Grace Read," the doctor said as he presented his companion to the two women.

"A pleasure to meet you," Sarah smiled.

"Are you enjoying your visit to Stickleback Hollow, Miss Hales?" Grace asked

"If it weren't for this interminable cold it would be a delightful time to visit," Jessica complained.

"What business takes you to see Old Woakes today?" the doctor asked, trying to change the subject.

"His fishing rod has been stolen; we are going to see if there is any assistance we can render," Sarah smiled.

"A more generous spirit I have never known. We won't keep you any longer, besides I need to get my sister out of the cold or else her complaining will be the death of me," the doctor chuckled and steered his sister away from the two women. Sarah and Grace watched them walk away from them for a few moments. When they were certain that the doctor and Miss Hales were out of earshot, Sarah turned to Grace and said,

"I wonder if she has any connection to the circus. Come, we should hurry, it will be getting dark soon."

The two women made their way down the street until they reached Old Woakes' cottage. It was a small place, but it was exceptionally neat and tidy. There was a small garden at the front of the house that had a small rose bush in it, but most of the garden was given over to growing vegetables.

In the summer, Old Woakes was often seen in his garden, tending to it, but with the snow covering the ground, you could only see the shape of the rose bush under the blanket of winter.

The front door was old and in need of a coat of paint, but it was still in good repair. There was an iron knocker on the door that moved easily as Grace used it to bang on the door.

It took Old Woakes a few minutes to make his way across his cottage to answer the door. When the door creaked open, Sarah and Grace were greeted by a morose face.

"Ah, Lady Sarah, my apologies, but I'm not fit to receive any visitors at the moment," Old Woakes muttered.

"We're sorry to call unannounced, but we came to talk to you about your fishing rod," Sarah explained.

"Ah, so you've heard it is missing. It's kind of you to take the trouble to come to me," Old Woakes managed to crack a slight smile and opened the door so that Sarah and Grace could step inside.

The cottage was as small inside as it appeared on the outside. The ceilings were low, and the beams that ran across it were made from oak. Anyone over 5"7' would struggle to walk around the place without banging their head.

There was a kettle on the fire that was whistling as Sarah and Grace both sat down on two of the stools that were close to the fire.

The cottage was in a state of disarray, clearly Old Woakes had pulled out all his belongings to search for his missing fishing rod.

"Constable Evans told us that you had reported your fishing rod had been stolen," Sarah said as Old Woakes limped over to take the kettle off the fire.

"Well, that is true, but I had been to the inn that night. I had a little bit too much Christmas cheer, and when I got back, it wasn't where I thought I left it." Old Woakes said with a small measure of embarrassment.

"Where do you think you left it?" Grace asked.

"I thought I left it in the small shed that's at the side of the cottage, but when I went in there the next day, it wasn't there. I've not seen it since," Old Woakes shrugged.

"But you put it away before you went to the inn?" Sarah asked.

"That's right. At least I thought I had. When I went to the shed to get my axe, it wasn't there. I went to Constable Evans, and he seemed to think that I'd done something with it when I came home from the inn. I've looked all over the house, and I can't find it," he explained.

"Do you lock the shed?" Sarah asked.

"Yes, the key is on a hook by the front door," Old Woakes replied.

"We won't trespass on your time any longer. The brigadier has a few fishing rods that I am sure he would be happy for you to have. I'll send one of the Baker boys over with them for you to choose whichever you like," Sarah smiled as she rose from beside the fire.

"Your ladyship is very kind," Old Woakes blushed and tugged at his forelock. He didn't like accepting charity, but he wasn't too proud to take a gift when a lady with such good standing offered it.

Sarah and Grace left Old Woakes cottage, leaving him to enjoy his tea in peace. Old Woakes settled down by his fire and felt a lot more relaxed than he had done for days.

It still puzzled him that his old fishing rod had disappeared, but knowing that Lady Sarah and the brigadier were keeping an eye on what was going on in the village made the old man feel better about the whole situation.

"Are we going back to Grangeback for the fishing rods?" Grace asked as she and Sarah walked back down the lane.

"Not yet, we need to visit the other people that reported stolen items first," Sarah replied.

"Then where are we going to next?" Grace sighed.

"The Reverend Butterfield should be walking by at any moment on his daily constitutional," Sarah smiled as she checked the time on the small gold pocket watch she had been given for Christmas.

It was a delicate piece of elegant clockwork on a fine chain. It had been made especially for Sarah by a jeweller in Chester. The outer casing of the water was engraved with

38

swallowtail butterflies fluttering around lotus flowers. On the inside, Sarah's name was engraved.

Sarah didn't know who the watch was from, but the butterflies and the lotus flowers reminded her of her home in India. It had only been a few months since Sarah had left India and come to England.

She still missed India. Though she was the daughter of an English Lady and an English Colonel, in her heart, she was a child of India. Though George was a kind and loving guardian, she missed her parents more with every day that passed. Though she loved the people of Stickleback Hollow and Grangeback, she missed the friends that she had left behind in India.

Every time she opened the watch, she thought about her old life and how she would, one day, go back to India.

"Here he comes now," Grace said, bringing Sarah back to the present. The Reverend Percy Butterfield was walking down the street towards the two women.

The reverend was a quiet man who enjoyed long walks, talking about cricket and sharing the bible with people. He was a good man who cared about the people of Stickleback Hollow. Every day, at the same time, he walked around the village so that anyone who needed to talk to him could find him easily.

He always took the same route. Some days he would be invited to join different people for tea. Sometimes it was because they needed spiritual counsel, whereas other times it was to discuss the value of a good defensive stroke.

Whatever the reason, Reverend Butterfield was well-liked in the village and not a soul in Stickleback Hollow, no matter how desperate, would have stolen from this man of the cloth.

"Good day, your ladyship, Miss Read, it isn't often I see the two of you walking around the village," the reverend greeted the two women cheerily.

"No, that's true. We are actually here in search of you, reverend," Sarah replied with a smile.

"Ah, and what can a humble servant of God do for such fine ladies?" Butterfield asked with a slight bow.

"We have been talking to Constable Evans about the items that have been disappearing around Stickleback Hollow," Sarah said.

"Ah, so you've taken it upon yourself to try and solve this little mystery. I suppose Arwyn told you about my candlestick going missing. I don't really think that anyone stole it, I only told Constable Evans about it because so many other people seemed to have lost things. I have been rather absent-minded recently, so I've probably put it away somewhere silly. It will turn up when I least expect it. I wouldn't spend too much time worrying about it, my lady. If you'll forgive me, I need to be back at the church for evensong," the reverend smiled and bid the two ladies good day before continuing on his way.

"Absent-minded indeed," Sarah muttered under her breath.

"Where to now, my lady?" Grace asked.

"Mr Christian lives at the end of the lane that is opposite the police house. It's not too far," Sarah replied. The two women set off down the lane, walking as briskly as they could in the snowy weather.

Not many people have travelled down the lane since the snow had fallen and no one had bothered to clear the lane as they had the main street in Stickleback Hollow.

The two women managed to avoid sliding about on hidden patches of ice and reached Mr Christian's home without incident.

"Is an old boot going missing really that important?" Grace whispered as they approached Mr Christian's door.

Grace was more than a little frightened of Mr Christian. He was a gruff man with a wild beard and even wilder eyebrows. He had a deep voice that seemed to completely dominate any space he was in.

When singing in church, his voice even managed to drown out the organ as well as the rest of the congregation.

He was a man that liked to keep to himself, which led to more than a few tall tales being told about him. In truth, Mr Christian was a retired missionary. He was the fifth son of a very good family in Yorkshire. His eldest brother had taken over the family estate, his other three brothers were commissioned in the army, but Mr Christian felt he was called to serve the church.

He had spent a lifetime travelling to some of the most uncivilised parts of the world and had become quite tired of the civilised world. But now he was too old to perform his duties, and he had retired to the parish of his friend Butterfield.

"It was important enough for Mr Christian to go to Constable Evans and report the loss of it," Sarah said firmly, as she knocked on the door.

"What? Who the devil is hammering on my door in this God-forsaken weather?" Mr Christian was talking to himself as he made his way to the front door; Grace was so terrified by the sound of his voice that she shrank to hide behind Sarah as the front door was flung open.

"Good day, Mr Christian," Sarah said as the huge man filled the doorway.

"Lady Sarah and Miss Read? What possible reason have you to travel to this odd corner of the village?" Mr Christian's voice echoed off the buildings and the trees.

"You've had an old boot stolen; I wanted to talk to you about it," Sarah replied.

"Well, Constable Evans certainly didn't want to talk about, but come in, come in," Mr Christian boomed, he stepped to one side and waved the two ladies inside.

The cottage was surprisingly neat but filled with strange curiosities from all the exotic countries that Mr Christian had visited. There were tribal masks, a mixture of weapons, pottery, weavings, carvings and paintings as well as silks and furniture that had no business being in the cottage of an English villager.

"What a marvellous collection you have," Sarah was clearly impressed by the items. Grace had scurried into the cottage behind Sarah was now wishing that she had remained in the snow.

The sight of so many alien things terrified her. She stood frozen to the spot in the hallway as Mr Christian led Sarah into the living room.

"Thank you, your ladyship, they are mostly trinkets that aren't worth very much, but each item has sentimental value. Can I offer you some tea?" Mr Christian asked, in the confines of the cottage, his voice wasn't anywhere near as overpowering as Grace expected it to be.

"What do you have?" Sarah asked.

"Well, as you are from India I can offer you Darjeeling, Assam or Nilgiri," Mr Christian smiled at the look of delight that spread over Sarah's face.

"Assam would be perfect, thank you," Sarah beamed.

"What about Miss Read?" Mr Christian asked. When no response came from the hallway, he looked at Sarah with a puzzled expression.

"Give her time, when she's ready, she'll come sit down. I'm sure she'll find Assam to be very exotic, but I have no doubt she'll enjoy it, once she's overcome her shock," Sarah tried her best not to giggle.

Mr Christian busied himself preparing tea as he spoke with Sarah.

"So you came about my missing boot," Mr Christian said as he took out his porcelain tea set.

"Yes, I was assuming that it was an old leather boot, but now I have seen your extensive collection, I imagine it was something considerably more valuable, Mr Christian," Sarah said as the leaves were spooned into the teapot.

"Please, call me James, your ladyship," Mr Christian insisted as he poured boiling water from the kettle of the dark tea leaves.

"If you will call me Sarah," she replied.

"Very well, Sarah, you are right, the boot that's missing is not an old leather boot. It's a small brass boot. It was made for me by some of the craftsmen at my last posting. You see, I only took one set of shoes with me to the jungle, and those shoes were a pair of walking boots. The villagers found them so strange, and I was always walking about in them. Boot was the first English word they learned, so when it came time for me to retire and I told them I was leaving, they gave me the boot," James explained as he carried the tea service over to where Sarah sat. As the two had been talking, Grace had crept into the doorway of the room.

She was still looking completely dumbfounded by her surroundings, but the sound of Mr Christian's voice no longer seemed to terrify her.

"So the boot has great sentimental value but very little physical worth?" Sarah asked as James handed her a cup, "Thank you, James."

"Indeed, it's not something I have lost as it hasn't been moved since I came to live here. So it must have been stolen. If there were a town watch still, it would already be back here, but that young policeman just told me it must have been lost," Mr Christian said gruffly.

"But there was no damage to your house or anything else in here?" Sarah asked.

"No, not a spot of dust out of place. The last time the boot was moved was when I took it to the jeweller in Chester to be cleaned. Come to think of it; there were some circus performers in there when I was there. Maybe they took a liking to it, and their acrobats slipped in through an open window to take it," James roared, causing Grace to disappear back into the hall.

Lady Sarah sat and sipped from her tea as she thought. Mr Christian kept trying to devise different scenarios in which circus performers managed to infiltrate the cottage unseen and abscond with the missing boot.

When the pot was empty, Grace was still hiding in the hall, and Mr Christian's theories about the robbery had become so wild that trained animals had become involved.

When it seemed that James had run out of ideas, Sarah thanked him for the tea, collected Grace from the hall and stepped back out onto the street.

Chapter 4

Mr Alexander Hunter had spent most of the morning touring the grounds of Grangeback with his hunting dog, Pattinson. By the early afternoon, he had reached the stables when he heard screeching coming from the hen house.

With Pattinson at his heels, Alex rushed round to see Cooky flapping about by the gate. The screeching sound was coming from the cook, who clearly upset about something.

"What is the matter, Cooky?" Mr Hunter asked as he reached the hen house.

"Oh, Mr Hunter! There were horrible children trying to get into the hens! I came out to get some eggs, and there they were! Their little paws were trying to lift the latches. I got such a fright. I screamed, and they ran off towards the village," Cooky cried.

"Who were they?" Alex asked as he took Cooky by the elbow and steered her towards the house.

"I don't know; I've never seen them before. Oh, Mr Hunter, please find out where they came from. I don't think my heart can take another fright like that," Cooky begged as Alex opened the door to the kitchen and took the alarmed cook inside.

"Cooky, whatever is wrong?" Mrs Bosworth asked.

"Oh, Mrs Bosworth, it was terrible!" Cooky cried as she collapsed into a chair.

"I'll go see Constable Evans. Cooky, it will all be fine. Pattinson, stay," Alex assured her as the cook began to tell Mrs Bosworth about her ordeal.

Mr Hunter didn't wait for a response from Cooky or Mrs Bosworth as he disappeared back through the door. Leaving the dog at the house meant that if the children chose to come back whilst he was down in the village, Pattinson could chase them off and would help Cooky to feel a little safer.

Mr Hunter hadn't seen any signs of anyone else on the property when he had been touring the grounds, but as he walked down to the village, he could see tracks that told him that several people had been creeping up towards the house from the village and only a handful of those tracks could belong to children.

The tracks went down to the village but rather than

leading Alex into Stickleback Hollow, they skirted the edge of the village and wended their way towards Duffleton Hall.

Rather than follow them alone, Mr Hunter made his way to the police house and knocked on the door.

"What now?" Arwyn demanded as he threw open the front door, "Oh, it's you Alex. Don't tell me, you're here to tell me something has been stolen," the constable sighed as he let Mr Hunter through the door.

"A lot of people have been reporting stolen items?" Alex asked as he walked into the sitting room.

"Yes, and Lady Sarah and Miss Read have been here to talk to me about it too," Arwyn sighed as he shook his head.

"Are you alright?" Alex asked with a bemused expression on his face.

"I'll be better when people stop losing things and call it being robbed," Arwyn said with frustration.

"Well, then you might not be very happy with what I have come to talk to you about," Alex replied.

"What?" Arwyn asked with a note of resignation in his voice.

"Cooky caught some children trying to break into the hen house at Grangeback. They ran off towards Stickleback

Hollow. I followed their tracks down to the edge of the village, but they veered off towards Duffleton Hall. I think they might have come from the circus that is setting up there," Mr Hunter explained.

"The circus? Did the children take anything or do any damage to the house?" the constable asked.

"No, Cooky's shrieking scared them off," Alex said with a wry smile curling at the corner of his mouth.

"I'm not surprised," Arwyn chuckled.

"Want some company?" Mr Hunter asked as Arwyn collected his cloak from the hallway.

"You aren't going to search for Lady Sarah?" Constable Evans asked as innocently as he could.

"If she came to talk to you about the stolen items, then she'll be busy investigating this latest mystery," Alex replied with a smile.

The two men stepped out into the cold after Constable Evans had extinguished the fire and the stove. He locked the door behind him, and the pair set off towards the circus camp.

They circled to the edge of the village where Alex had last seen the tracks of the children and picked up the trail.

Though Mr Hunter suspected that the children came

from the circus camp, it was only sensible to follow the tracks and make certain. Sure enough, all the tracks led to the circus camp and disappeared amongst the carriages and canvas tents.

As the two men approached the circus camp, there was a sudden flurry of activity. They were spotted by two women that were doing their washing at the edge of the camp. The moment they laid eyes on the constable and the hunter, the women dropped their washing and disappeared into the nearest tent.

Moments later, a man that was easily a full head and shoulders taller than Mr Hunter stepped out. He had a bald head but an impressive moustache and beard as well as muscles, the likes of which neither Arwyn or Alex had ever seen.

He was followed by a man that was a much more normal size with long ginger hair and mutton chops that grew across his upper lip to form a moustache.

Behind him was a third man that was rather small in size with short brown hair. He looked very unassuming, but from the way he walked and carried himself both Arwyn and Alex made a mental note to keep at least an arms distance from him at all times.

"I'm sorry, but we don't let visitors walk around our camp. The shows will be held on New Year's Day, gentleman," the ginger man said in a loud voice as he walked towards Alex and Arwyn.

"And who are you?" Mr Hunter asked.

"I am Bairstow, ringmaster and owner of this fine circus. Who are you?" the ginger man replied curtly.

"Mr Hunter, gamekeeper for the Grangeback estate. This is Constable Evans from Stickleback Hollow," Alex said coldly.

"And what would bring you to the circus?" the tall man asked.

"Some children tried to break into the hen house on the Grangeback Estate. The cook caught them, and we followed their tracks back here," Alex looked the tall man up and down as he spoke, evaluating whether he was just strong or if he was going to be fast as well.

The small man didn't say a word, but listened to the exchange that was being conducted. At the moment the children were mentioned, he turned and walked into the camp, returning a few minutes later, dragging two boys by their ears.

"Say it," he growled at the two boys as he brought them to stand in front of Alex and Arwyn.

"Oww, we didn't -" one of the boys protested, but his sentence turned into a cry of pain as the small man twisted his ear.

"Alright! We're sorry. We won't go up to the house again!" the other boy cried.

"Why were you up at the house in the first place?" Arwyn asked.

"We wouldn't clean up after the elephant, so we weren't given any breakfast. We went to the big house to see if we could beg some food, but there was the hen house so we thought we'd just go and take some eggs." the first boy replied.

The small man let go of their ears and clouted both boys across the back of the head.

"You don't go stealing from people. You steal, and we won't be welcome back. We can't put on shows, none of us eat. You remember that," the small man barked at the two boys.

"If that's everything, good day gentlemen, we hope

54

you'll come to see the show," Bairstow said.

Arwyn glanced at Alex, who nodded. The two men turned and walked away from the camp. The circus performers didn't move from where they stood, making sure that the constable and the hunter were both gone before they returned to what they were doing.

"Did you get the feeling they were trying to hide something?" Arwyn asked as the two men entered the trees around Stickleback Hollow, well out of earshot of the circus.

"A show of force and giving up the two boys like that? They're hiding something," Alex sighed.

"I'm beginning to think that maybe all these items going missing in the Hollow aren't people being careless after all," the constable said thoughtfully.

"I'll keep an eye on them; see if anything else suspicious happens," Alex replied.

"I'll try and find out where Bairstow's circus has been before and whether there were any thefts that are similar to the ones I've had reported," Arwyn said.

"I think it's best you don't mention this to Sarah though." Alex cautioned the constable.

Chapter 5

By the time Grace had recovered from the shock and was able to speak again, the two women had arrived at the home of Miss Gunn.

Miss Gunn was the daughter of a lay preacher and had spent most of her life as a governess to one family or another. When her father had died there had been a small legacy for her that had enabled her to buy a small cottage in Stickleback Hollow and still had some money remaining to live on.

Miss Gunn didn't live on her own though, her niece, Miss Beaumont, lived with her. She was also a governess, so she didn't live with Miss Gunn all of the time, but it was still her home.

Miss Beaumont was currently at one of the estates in Kent, so Miss Gunn was on her own. She welcomed Sarah and Grace into her home and took them to sit by the small fire she had going.

"It was good of you to come, your ladyship, but the young constable is probably right. I have just put the fork down somewhere. It will turn up," Miss Gunn said kindly.

"Was it just a fork that went missing?" Grace asked.

"It was the silver fork I was given by the last family I worked for when I left their service. It isn't much to look at, but it is something that I am sad to have misplaced," Miss Gunn replied.

"Where did you keep it, Miss Gunn?" Sarah asked.

"It was on the window sill of the kitchen that overlooks the road. I remember that the last time I saw it, the latch on the window was a little loose. Mr Cartwright came and fixed it for me yesterday. Every time there was a breeze, the window would be blown open," Miss Gunn told the ladies enthusiastically.

Grace chatted to Miss Gunn about her time as a governess for about half an hour whilst Sarah listened. When Sarah had felt they had spent sufficient time being polite, she bid Miss Gunn good day.

Outside, the light was quickly fading from the sky.

"We should go back to the house; it will be too dark to ride soon," Grace insisted.

"You're right. We'll visit with Wilson, Mr.Claydon and Miss Roy tomorrow," Sarah agreed reluctantly.

The lamps had all been lit by the time Sarah and Grace arrived back at Grangeback. They were greeted by Bosworth and the tale of the drama of the children trying to break into the hen house.

Sarah spent the evening thinking about what she had been told by each of the villagers she had spoken too whilst Grace played the Brigadier at cards.

Cooky was still clucking about the hen house and was begging Bosworth to set a guard of footmen around her precious chickens during the night.

Sarah went to bed early, but she didn't sleep. Instead, she lay in her bed, her new pocket watch on the pillow beside her.

She thought about her father's pocket watch. She had discovered that it was missing from the things that Sarah had that once belonged to her parents.

She hadn't told anyone that she had discovered that it was missing. Sarah was sure that either Alex or George had removed it and hidden it somewhere, but it didn't stop the theft of the watch from hurting. The pocket watch had been something special to her father, and in lieu of having her family there, she had her memories and their possessions.

Whoever gave her the delicate pocket watch that she was now fixated on, understood the pain that she felt, even if she never voiced it aloud.

As the candle flickered and caused the butterflies to dance over the lotus flowers, tears ran down Sarah's cheeks until she was so exhausted from grief that she fell asleep, the pocket watch clutch firmly in her hand.

The next morning Sarah set out without Grace for company. All the time walking around in the cold had left Grace with a high fever.

Doctor Hales was sent for, and Mrs Bosworth fussed over Grace, making sure that a large fire was set in her bedroom and that she was tucked up in a thick nest of blankets.

Sarah was glad of the time to ride down to the village on her own. She walked down to the stables and found that she was not the only person to be awake early and looking forward to riding.

"Good morning, your ladyship," Mr Hunter greeted her as she stepped into the stable yard.

"Good morning, Mr Hunter," Sarah replied.

"Miss Read isn't with you?" Alex asked breezily, as he

placed Harald's saddle on the stable door.

"No, she has a fever, so Mrs Bosworth is treating her like a newborn calf," Sarah replied, "Where are the stable boys?"

"They don't get up for another hour yet," Alex laughed, "I hope Miss Read feels better soon. Have you sent for the doctor?"

"He's on his way," Sarah yawned and rubbed her eyes.

"What's wrong?" Alex asked as he stopped and looked at Sarah.

"Nothing," Sarah tried to assure him, but Mr Hunter fixed her with a withering look, "I didn't sleep very well," she admitted.

"What kept you awake?" Alex asked as he walked over to stand in front of her. Sarah looked up at him and considered her words carefully before she answered.

"The pocket watch that belonged to my father; it isn't amongst his belongings. Do you know where it is?" she asked quietly.

"Yes," he replied.

"Will you tell me where it is?" Sarah asked.

"No," Alex said softly. Sarah closed her eyes and took a

deep breath.

"Please, you don't need to protect me," she whispered.

"Sarah, you may not understand it, but I do need to protect you. Not for your sake, but for mine." Alex gently replied as he tilted her chin upwards.

"Did you have a gold pocket watch made for me?" Sarah asked, opening her eyes and looking at Alex.

"Yes," he sighed.

"Alex -" Sarah began, but Alex stepped back from her.

"We've been through this before. I won't ruin you," Alex said abruptly.

"You won't ruin me, but you will protect me as though I belong to you?" Sarah asked hotly.

"I protect you because I love you and I can't go through the pain of losing someone else that I love. I went to Scotland to try and free myself of you, but I can't. You are so engrained in my being that it physically hurts not to be near you. I won't ruin you because I love you and I won't make you the subject of gossip and scandal. I won't turn you into a social pariah. I won't have our children go through what I endured at school. No woman I have ever met or ever will meet will be as frustrating and exhilarating as you are -" Alex yelled until

61

Sarah threw her arms around him and buried her face in his chest.

Her shoulders were shaking as she cried, and Alex could hear slight sobs and sniffs as Sarah tried to control herself.

"I'm sorry," Sarah sobbed. Mr Hunter gently folded his arms around her, one hand softly stroking her hair.

"You haven't any need to be," Alex replied.

"You don't understand. I'm sorry that you were treated so badly at school and that our children will go through the same thing," Sarah sniffed.

"Your family will disown you; you can't -" Alex protested. Sarah tilted her head up from his chest and kissed him. It was a fleeting brush of her lips on his that caught Alex completely by surprise.

"George won't disown me," Sarah breathed.

"Your family in London -" Alex began, but Sarah kissed him again. This time she let her lips linger on his for a moment.

"They are my family in name only; they have no bearing on my life," she replied.

"Your reputation, your good standing, you'll never be

invited to any social event -" Alex continued to try and argue. When Sarah kissed him this time, he kissed her back.

"We can hide in the house, in the lodge, in the woods, we can travel the world and meet new and interesting people that are so far beyond the tiny and confining social circles of England," she argued back.

"I love you," Mr Hunter said as he stroked her face.

"I know," Lady Montgomery Baird Watson-Wentworth smiled and shivered slightly, "Where is Pattinson?"

"He's guarding Cooky and the henhouse," Alex laughed as he pulled Sarah closer to him to keep her warm.

"Where are you going this morning?" she asked.

"To ride around the grounds, make sure that everything is as it should be. Where are you going?" he replied.

"Into Stickleback Hollow to visit Wilson, Mr Claydon and Miss Roy," Sarah answered.

"They won't be awake yet. You should go back to bed and get some sleep," Mr Hunter told her.

"It won't help," she replied.

"Have you talked to anyone about it? Your parents'

deaths, I mean," he asked cautiously.

"No, did you talk to anyone about your mother's death?" Sarah asked.

"No, but I was angry for a long time, and I took out that anger on others very unfairly. I don't want you to make that mistake," Alex admitted.

"If I want to talk about it, will you listen?" Sarah asked nervously.

"Come to the lodge; we can walk, you can talk and then when we get there you can lie down and sleep," Alex smiled at her.

The two set off through the snow. George stood at his window and smiled as he saw the two figures making their way across the lawn, arm-in-arm.

By the time they reached the lodge, Sarah felt as though a weight had been lifted from her shoulders and was completely exhausted. She was so tired that Alex had to carry her up the stairs. He took her to the room that had once belonged to his mother and placed her gently down on the bed.

"Alex," Sarah called out as Mr Hunter made to leave the room.

"Yes?" he paused and looked back at her.

"Don't leave," she said sleepily. Alex cocked his head and smiled at her.

"What do you want me to do?" he asked.

"Hold me," she replied.

Chapter 6

When Sarah woke up, she found that she wasn't alone. Alex was lying beside her with his arms wrapped around her.

"What time is it?" she asked sleepily.

"About ten o'clock." Mr Hunter replied as Sarah reached up and gently ran her fingers over his cheek.

"When do you need to ride around the estate?" she asked.

"It can wait," he said as he kissed her fingers, "When do you need to visit Wilson, Claydon and Miss Roy?" he asked.

"It can wait," she whispered softly and gently kissed him. Mr Hunter responded to her with more passion than Sarah had expected. The gentle embrace was replaced with something more urgent.

She gasped as she felt his hand move slowly down from her back to her hip, pulling her body towards his, his firm grip awaking something in Sarah that she had never experienced before.

She wrapped her fingers in his hair as he rolled her onto her back. Her heart was pounding in her chest as he gazed down at her with adoring eyes.

"If this is truly what you want, then I am yours," he whispered. Sarah gulped and nodded.

"It is what I want," she replied nervously. Alex brushed the hair away from her face with his fingertips.

"Have you ever?" he asked.

"No. Have you?" Sarah felt a strange mixture of terror and desire as she looked up at him.

"Yes," Alex replied. She had thought that the idea of him sharing the bed of another woman would hurt, but she felt oddly relieved as he spoke.

"Will it hurt?" she asked.

"Possibly, but I will be gentle. If it hurts too much, I will stop," he assured her as he leaned his forehead against hers and slipped his knee between her legs.

"All right." Sarah breathed. Alex brushed his lips against hers, and Sarah felt his hand move from her hip to the buttons on her jodhpurs. As he undid them, Sarah found her hands moving to the buttons on the shirt that Mr Hunter wore.

When the last of the buttons were undone, Sarah slipped the shirt off his shoulders. Alex stood up suddenly. For a moment, Sarah felt panicked by the idea that she had done something wrong. Mr Hunter paused and smiled at her before removing the rest of his clothes.

Sarah began to try and quickly remove hers.

"Don't," Alex softly breathed in her ear, taking hold of her hands as he climbed back onto the bed, "Let me."

He slowly undid and removed all of her clothes; Sarah felt the pleasure of anticipation slowly take control of every part of her body. She lay on the bed as he looked down at her naked body.

"Are you ready?" he asked. Sarah nodded in reply, not trusting herself to speak. Alex slowly crawled up the bed; between her legs. He slowly slipped into her. Sarah bit her lip to keep from crying out.

Each thrust brought a wave of pain that was more exquisitely satisfying than Sarah could ever have imagined. She began to moan and dug her fingernails into his shoulders. Her body began to move in the same rhythm as his.

Each moan that escaped Sarah's lips served to

encourage Alex. He began to thrust more aggressively, his hands gripping her slight body closer to him. His mouth went in search of hers; barely managing to stifle her moaning that grew louder with each passing second.

He felt her legs wrapping around his waist, the tight grip of her thighs urging him to push harder and deeper. He felt her lips on his neck and responded by biting hers.

Sarah called out his name and begged for more. All gentleness had been swept away by passion. He was so lost in his desire for her, and she was overwhelmed by levels of ecstasy that she had never experienced before.

Alex fought to control his release until he was certain that Sarah's pleasure had reached its climax.

The pair lay collapsed with exhaustion amongst the sheets. Sarah turned her head to look at Alex.

"Again?" she asked with a smile on her face. Alex looked at her and laughed.

"Give me a minute," he replied, wrapping her in his arms and drawing her to him.

It was evening before Sarah and Alex stirred from the lodge. Mr Hunter didn't want Sarah to leave, but they both knew that if she didn't return to Grangeback that men would be sent out to look for her.

"I love you," Alex whispered to her as he walked her back to the main house.

"You don't want to tell anyone about this, do you?" Sarah asked as she leaned her head on Alex's shoulder.

"I know that I love you and that nothing in this world will change how I feel, but I also know that you have been ripped from everything that you had ever known and landed in the middle of an alien land. How you feel now may change and -"

"You don't want to ruin me," Sarah finished Alex's sentence for him, "You are such a fool, Mr Hunter. But a fool I am in love with. If you don't want people to know, then it shall be our secret for now."

"Thank you," Alex said with relief and kissed the top of her head.

"Though I wouldn't wait too long if I were you, now that it has spread around the neighbourhood that I have refused Daniel, other young men will be lining up at the door," Sarah teased.

"And I am sure that Pattinson could drive them all off single pawed," Alex replied.

As the couple drew within sight of the house, they broke apart, just in case anyone was looking out of a window.

"Oh, Lady Sarah! I am so glad your back. I was beginning to worry," Cooky clucked as Sarah and Alex entered the kitchen.

"I'm sorry Cooky, Mr Hunter and I were touring the grounds," Sarah apologised as Pattinson bounded over to greet the pair.

"What on earth happened to your neck, my lady?" Cooky asked. Sarah had tried to cover the bite mark that Alex had left on her neck with her hair, but had been unsuccessful.

"Oh, I got stung by some form of insect in the woods," Sarah lied as she rubbed her hand over the mark.

"You should go see Doctor Hales in the morning; it looks a rather nasty bite," Cooky said with concern.

"Speaking of the doctor, how is Miss Read?" Alex asked, desperately trying to change the subject.

"Not well at all, the doctor says she has a terrible cold. She's going to be tucked up in bed for days. If you go in to visit her, you must wear a mask so that you don't get sick too," Cooky replied sternly.

"I'll make sure I remember that. Thank you for your

time today, Mr Hunter," Sarah said, turning to Alex.

"It was my pleasure, my lady," Alex replied with a slight smirk on his face. Sarah blushed a deep scarlet, but fortunately Cooky wasn't paying any attention to the pair, "Goodnight, Cooky. Come Pattinson, time we were getting home."

Mr Hunter left, and Sarah made her way up the stairs to her room.

"Good evening, my dear." the brigadier greeted Sarah on the landing.

"George, you startled me!" Sarah cried and clamped her hand over the mark on her neck.

"My apologies, Sarah, you must have been rather distracted not to hear me stomping about," the brigadier chuckled.

"Just thinking over the events of the day," Sarah laughed nervously. George looked at her for a moment and shook his head.

"You are terrible at behaving in a natural manner when you have a secret to keep. My wife and daughter were just the same," he chided her.

"I don't know what you are talking about," Sarah tried

to sound as breezy as she could, but George fixed her with a hard stare.

"Come with me," he said sternly. Sarah felt her stomach drop as she obediently followed George to his study.

George shut the door and motioned for Sarah to sit in the chair opposite his desk. He sat at his desk and leaned on it as he spoke.

"Sarah, you are a young woman with a rather stubborn disposition, but I am your guardian, and I expect you to be honest with me," George said firmly.

"Brigadier -" Sarah began to protest, but George held up his hand to silence her.

"Where have you been today?" he asked.

"With Mr Hunter," Sarah replied.

"Doing what?" George continued his questioning. Sarah opened her mouth to reply but closed it again almost instantly, "Well?"

"I can't say," Sarah replied, dropping her eyes to look at the desk.

"And why not?" George asked, raising his voice.

"Because I promised to keep it secret," Sarah replied, feeling more and more wretched by the second.

"And how did you get that mark on your neck?" George asked. Sarah remained silent causing the brigadier to lose what remained of his temper,

"Sarah, whatever you have been doing today, I don't believe for one second you were with Alex. There is no possible circumstance that my son would ask you to keep whatever you have been doing secret or result in you having an injury like that," George roared.

"Your son?" Sarah asked with wide eyes as she looked up at her guardian.

"What?" George was so taken aback by the question that he forgot to be angry.

"Alex is *your* son?" Sarah asked in disbelief.

"Don't change the subject. I want to know where you have been," George tried to regain control of the conversation.

"I've been making love to your son. He's the one that gave me this mark," Sarah replied crossly.

"Are you mad? What do you, who do, how -" the colour drained from George's face as Sarah glared at him.

"I love him, and he loves me, only he thinks he is too far beneath me in social standing to matter. He's the son of a gentleman, making him a gentleman, but he doesn't know that

74

because you've never told him that he's your son!" Sarah hissed.

"So you took him to bed?" George hissed back.

"What about his mother?" Sarah fired back.

"Are you going to marry him?" George demanded.

"Are you going to tell him he's your son?" Sarah asked.

"Do you honestly love him?" George frowned.

"Yes," Sarah replied.

"Truly?" George asked again.

"Yes," Sarah replied curtly.

"I'll talk to him tomorrow," George said, closing his eyes. Sarah stood from the chair and went to leave the study.

"If I didn't love him, would you ever have told him?" she asked.

"No, I wouldn't," George admitted.

Chapter 7

The next day, Mr Hunter was awake early than usual. He wanted to tour the grounds before anyone in Grangeback would be up. He left Pattinson sleeping on the foot of his bed.

By the time he reached the main house, it was still dark, and only the servants were awake. He stole in through the French windows of the drawing room and made his way up to Sarah's room.

As Grace was to be confined to her bed with a cold, Alex was certain that Sarah would be alone. None of the servants saw him as he stole through the house and crept into Sarah's room.

The lady was lying on her bed with the gold pocket watch clutched firmly in her hand. Mr Hunter perched on the edge of her bed, and gently brushed the hair off her face.

Sarah stirred from her slumber and smiled when she saw the hunter. He leaned in and kissed her.

"Good morning," he whispered.

"I missed you last night," Sarah replied as she stroked the back of his neck.

"I'm here now," Alex smiled.

"Did you miss me?" Sarah asked.

"More than I can tell," he replied.

"Show me instead," she told him.

Mr Hunter didn't need to be asked twice. The two made love, trying to be as quiet as possible in case any of the servants were walking past her room.

"You know, it is much easier to undress you when you're wearing your nightgown," Alex whispered as he held her naked body next to his.

"You'll find it even easier with my summer dresses." Sarah teased.

"I will have to be more careful about where I leave marks in future though," Alex said as he kissed her neck, slowly moving down her body to her breasts, "maybe here would be a better place."

"Only you will see them," Sarah said as she ran her fingers through his hair.

"I'm glad to hear it. But the question is: will you enjoy it as much as me biting your neck?" he said, moving his hands up her body towards her breasts.

"I find the thought of it rather exhilarating," she smiled as she closed her eyes, enjoying the sensation of his fingers moving over her body.

"I thought that Cooky knew for certain what we had been doing all day when she saw the mark. I'm glad that it was her that saw it and not anyone else," Alex said.

"George saw it as well. He has something he wants to talk to you about," Sarah said, opening her eyes and looking down at Alex.

"He can talk to me later. By my reckoning, we still have half an hour before one of the maids will come to get you out of bed, and before they do, I intend to leave a few more marks," Mr Hunter replied.

As predicted, half an hour later, a maid knocked on Sarah's door to help her dress. Alex had already left the room and snuck downstairs to wait for Sarah in the drawing room, only to find the brigadier there instead.

"I had a feeling you might be here early this morning, though clearly you arrived earlier than I anticipated," George frowned at the hunter. Alex felt his cheeks flush.

"What do you mean?" Alex asked.

"Sit down, my boy, I know about you and Sarah," George sighed.

"And you disapprove?" Mr Hunter asked.

"Yes and no. I don't disapprove of the two of you being in love; I don't think there has ever been a pair that are as well-matched as the two of you. I disapprove of how you are conducting yourselves. It will only lead to scandal. Though I suppose there is something brave about your behaviour. Either neither of you care about what people will think –which is rather brave - or you are both too stupid to have thought of it," George replied, shaking his head.

"It's the former," Alex assured him.

"Then you are both far braver than I ever was. I have something I have to tell you, my boy, something that I have kept from you for a very long time because I feared the scandal that would come from it being made public," George told him with a note of resignation.

"Oh?" Alex frowned.

"I know who your father is," George said.

"Who?" Alex asked, jumping to his feet.

"I am," George said slowly. Mr Hunter stared at the brigadier.

"You? Why did you never tell? All these years, all this time!" Alex felt completely betrayed. He had always looked up to the brigadier as a father figure and wondered why the old man had always taken such good care of him.

"My pride," George replied helplessly.

"Then why tell me now?" Alex demanded.

"Because you love Sarah," the brigadier replied.

"You think that I need to be recognised as your son to be worthy of her?" Mr Hunter asked crossly.

"No, it's not what I think that's important. It's everyone else. I want the two of you to be happy together," George tried to calm Alex down.

"We can only be happy if I am recognised as your son?" Alex frowned.

"Please, Alex, I know this is unexpected and something that is difficult to hear, but try to understand. I have only ever wanted what was best for you," George pleaded with him. Mr Hunter looked at the brigadier coldly. There were a myriad of emotions swirling around inside as he stood in the study. He couldn't even begin to explain how he felt, nor did he feel that he was under any obligation to articulate those feelings.

"Please, say something," George said after the silence

had been dragged out for longer than the brigadier was comfortable with.

But Mr Hunter didn't say a word; instead, he turned, left the study and walked back to the lodge, still unable to voice what he was feeling.

George sat in his study with his head in his hands for over an hour before Sarah found him.

"Are you alright?" she asked as she affectionately touched his shoulder.

"No, my dear, I am about as far from alright as I have ever been," George replied sadly.

Sarah was torn between trying to comfort George and going in search of Alex. George had a household full of trusted servants and his friend the doctor to call upon. Mr Hunter had Pattinson.

Sarah made her way down to the lodge, following the tracks that Alex had left in the snow. She slipped round to the back door and went into the small house.

Alex was sat on the floor, staring at the fire he had built in the small grate. Pattinson was sat beside him, the dog was resting his head on Alex's leg and whined at Sarah as she moved across the floor to sit beside him.

She didn't say a word as she leaned her head on his shoulder and wrapped her arms about his arm. They sat on the floor, silently, until the fire had burned down to its embers.

"Can you forgive him?" Sarah was the one to break the silence.

"I don't know," Mr Hunter sighed.

"Whatever you decide, it doesn't change who you are, and it doesn't change how I feel or what we agreed," Sarah replied. She gently kissed his cheek and then attempted to build a new fire in the grate.

Alex watched the young lady for a few minutes as she struggled with the logs. He started chuckling at the sight of her carefully placing the smallest logs she could find in a ring around the edge of the embers.

"What?" Sarah asked as she turned to look at the hunter.

"That's not how you build a fire," he grinned.

"Then you do it," Sarah said, holding out the logs towards Alex.

"How about I teach you instead?" he asked.

When Sarah arrived back at Grangeback, it was still

early in the afternoon. Alex had wanted to be alone with his thoughts and had walked up to Swallow's End with Pattinson to think things through.

George was refusing to leave his study, and the whole household had become subdued by his mood. Only Mrs Bosworth and Sarah knew what had happened, but the effect of his mood on the household was palpable.

"Oh! Lady Sarah! You must talk to Grace. She's refusing to stay in bed and arguing with Mrs Bosworth," Cooky flapped.

"Where are they?" Sarah sighed.

"In the library," Cooky replied.

Chapter 8

Grace refused to stay in bed, and nothing the doctor, Sarah or Mrs Bosworth could say would change her mind.

Sarah decided that the best thing to do was to take Grace out of the house and away from the tense atmosphere of the house. After breakfast, Sarah ordered the carriage to take them down to the village.

Grace might not want to stay in bed, but that didn't mean that Sarah was going to let her go marching about in the snow when there was a warm carriage to ride in.

The two women sat in silence as the carriage rolled down to the village. Sarah was lost in her thoughts about Alex, and Grace was using most of her energy to keep herself upright in her seat.

Sarah had instructed the driver to deliver them to Mr Claydon's home first. Mitchell Claydon lived in one of the largest homes in the village of Stickleback Hollow. It had once been three cottages that all stood close together, but it was now something of a sprawling townhouse.

He was an explorer of some renown and had even been sent on a handful of expeditions by the king. He was a big man who looked like he would be more at home in a boxing ring than a sleepy village in the heart of Cheshire, but the man seemed to enjoy the quiet of the countryside, and abhorred the noise and life of London.

He was one of the few residents of Stickleback Hollow that Sarah hadn't met in her short tenure at Grangeback. He mostly kept to himself, and whenever there were large events in the village, he made sure that he was elsewhere.

Mr Hunter spoke of him with high regard, so Sarah didn't feel anxious as she knocked on the front door of the cottage complex.

A towering man with a young face, quick smile and kind eyes opened the door.

"Mr Claydon, I presume?" Sarah said as she looked up at the giant man.

"The infamous Lady Montgomery Baird Watson-Wentworth, what brings you to my door?" Mr Claydon replied with a broad grin.

"Your missing pocket knife," Sarah replied.

"Hunter didn't exaggerate," Mr Claydon laughed, "Please come in out of the cold," he said warmly.

Sarah had the driver bring Grace into the house and placed her in front of the fire whilst she sat and talked to Mr Claydon.

"Mr Hunter told you about me?" Sarah asked as they sat down.

"Half the village has tales to tell of you. It's a pleasure to have another adventurous individual in the neighbourhood. I'm sure you have many stories you could tell me about your life in India, but they can be saved for another day. You came to ask about my pocket knife," Mr Claydon replied.

"Yes, you went to Constable Evans and told him it had been stolen," Sarah said, folding her hands in her lap.

"It must have been a pickpocket, and a very skilled pickpocket at that. I had it when I was helping cut some rope for two boys from the circus camp. I put it back in my pocket, came home through the village and found it was missing a few hours later," Mr Claydon explained.

"I see. Was there anything special about this pocket knife?" Sarah asked.

"Nothing particularly remarkable. It has been with me

on all of my adventures though, so it is more of a companion than a tool to me. The constable suggested that it could have simply fallen out of my pocket, but after being washed down rapids and chased through the jungle by cannibals without it going missing, I find it hard to believe that a walk down the main street in Stickleback Hollow could dislodge it from its home," Mr Claydon said with a raised eyebrow.

"It does seem a little unlikely," Sarah agreed.

"I suppose that other people have had items go missing to bring you to my door," Mr Claydon said.

"They have, it's quite an interesting array of items," Sarah smiled.

"Well, then you best get to searching!" Mr Claydon grinned.

It was a brief visit, but Sarah found she liked Mr Claydon. Part of her wanted to stay longer and to discuss the different wonders that he had seen across the globe, but there were more pressing things to attend to for the moment.

Sarah whisked Grace away from the fire and back to the carriage. It was a short journey to their next destination, but Sarah wanted to keep Grace out of the cold as much as she possibly could.

It was Miss Roy that the ladies went to call on next. The home of Miss Millie Roy was a complete contrast to that of Mr Claydon.

The cottage was easily the smallest dwelling in Stickleback Hollow and was in a very sorry state of repair.

Miss Roy was a charwoman, though she was only just a woman. She had come to the village just before Sarah had. Her arrival had been sudden and rather strange, and almost nothing was known about her past.

She was such an enigma that some of the inhabitants of Stickleback Hollow had created stories about what had brought Miss Roy to the village.

Some said she was the illegitimate daughter of the king that had been forced into hiding for fear that she would try to steal the throne from the newly crowned queen. Others said that she was the daughter of a lord that had fled from her father to avoid being married to an undesirable man.

Then there were those that felt the other half of the village spent far too much time inventing fairy tales instead of working.

Millie Roy worked hard for the small amount of money she was paid. She didn't complain about the hours that she had to work or the poverty that she lived in. She always seemed to be in a cheerful mood as well.

For a girl that earned so little, Sarah felt it was rather odd that she owned something as expensive as a pearl broach.

"Lady Sarah!" Millie said with surprise as she opened the door to her house.

"Millie, Constable Evans said that you told him you'd had something stolen," Sarah said as Millie beckoned Grace and Sarah into the house.

"Yes, a small pearl broach. It was a gift from my father." Millie said.

"Where did you keep?" Sarah asked.

"Normally, it was in a box that I hide under the floorboards, but I was wearing it when it was taken," Millie said sadly.

"You were wearing it?" Grace asked groggily.

"Yes, one Mr Gordon Hales asked me to go for a walk with him on Christmas Eve. I wanted to try and impress him, so I wore all my finest things and pinned the broach to my cloak. He told me how lovely it was almost straight away. When I got home it was missing though," Millie started to cry.

"It's okay, Millie," Sarah soothed.

"You don't understand! It's the only thing I have left from my father. He was such a kind man," Millie sobbed.

Sarah knew how Millie felt, but she didn't know what to say to the girl.

"I'll stay with Millie for a bit," Grace said as she slipped her arm around Millie's shoulders.

"I will go see Wilson. I'll leave the carriage for you, whenever you are ready, you can go back to Grangeback. I'll walk," Sarah agreed and left the two girls alone.

She felt rather relieved to be on her own and able to walk the short distance back to the inn.

Wilson was stood behind the bar, looking his normal, cheery self. There wasn't much that he could tell Sarah about the missing tankard. He wasn't even sure how long it had been missing.

"I just looked up one day, and it wasn't hanging on its hook." Wilson shrugged. Before Sarah could question him any further about the tankard, the door to the inn was thrown open, and Constable Evans strode in, wearing a face of thunder.

"Wilson, beer," was all he said as he sat down at the bar.

"What's wrong, Arwyn?" Sarah frowned.

"Miss Baker, she's threatening to write to the chief constable because I haven't found her stupid leather tools and all the other items that people have lost," Constable Evans growled as Wilson put a bottle of beer down in front of him.

"Why would she do that?" Sarah asked.

"Why? Because she's heard that you've been asking people about their missing items and telling them that I'm wrong!" Arwyn cried.

Though Sarah hadn't been trying to tarnish Constable Evans' reputation, it was clear that she had overstepped her bounds in what she had said to some of the complainants.

"I'm sorry, Arwyn, I didn't mean to get you in trouble," Sarah apologised.

"I know you didn't. You just can't help being nosy," Constable Evans said, shaking his head.

"Well, you know the gentry, we can't help ourselves," Sarah shrugged.

Arwyn laughed slightly and took a swig from the bottle of beer.

Outside the inn, there was the sound of shouting, music and carriages trundling by.

"I wonder what that is," Sarah said as she made her way towards the door.

"See, off again, being nosy," Arwyn said, shaking his head.

Sarah opened the door to the inn and stepped out into the street. People were coming out of their houses and the shops to watch a rather strange procession going by.

It was the circus performers. They were calling out to the crowd, telling them about what the circus had and when the shows were going to be held.

For many people, it was the most exotic thing that they would ever see, and the most impressive thing was the elephant.

It walked in the middle of the procession and trumpeted as it went. The ground shook under its huge feet, and the people of Stickleback Hollow were held in rapture by it.

Wilson, Emma, and Arwyn had all come out to look when Sarah didn't come back.

"Well, I never thought I'd live to see something like that," Wilson said with awe as he gazed at the elephant.

Sarah stayed silent. The elephant was an Asian

elephant and something she had seen many times. She had even ridden them when she was growing up in India.

The sight of the elephant brought a tear to her eye and a stab of pain to her heart.

"Oh, those boys are with the circus, they came in to drink with an older woman a few days before Christmas," Emma said as she spotted them amongst the performers that were with the elephant.

"They're a strange bunch, Mr Hunter and I went to visit them the other day after two boys tried to get into the hen house at Grangeback. They were acting very suspiciously," Arwyn said.

"Never trust travelling folk. They keep far too much to themselves," Wilson said gruffly.

"Come to think of it, quite a few things started to go missing after the circus arrived on the land of Duffleton Hall," Emma said thoughtfully.

"Probably coincidence," Arwyn shrugged, but Sarah wasn't so certain.

Chapter 9

The arrival of Captain Jonnes Smith in Stickleback Hollow was never a welcome sight. It wasn't that the man was unpopular or an unpleasant man, but wherever Captain Jonnes Smith went, upheaval was never too far away.

He was the chief constable of the Cheshire Constabulary, and it was only the most serious of matters that brought him to visit with Constable Evans.

When Arwyn opened the door of the police house, his heart stopped. His first thought was that Miss Baker had followed through with her threat to write to the chief constable, but it soon became apparent that something more serious than missing leather tools had brought Captain Jonnes Smith to call.

"Evans, I need you to find someone," the chief constable barked as he marched past Arwyn and into the police house.

"Who, sir?"

"Paul Curran. He's a wastrel, a scoundrel and he

attacked several people in Chester on 23rd December. We've been looking for him in every village between the city and the border of the county. So far we've not found any sign of him, but there's a possibility he's with the circus that Lord Cooper is playing host to," Captain Jonnes Smith explained.

"Have you got a description of the man?" Arwyn asked.

"Yes, he's a stocky man, not too tall, dark hair, no beard or moustache and has a vicious snarl," the chief constable said.

"I'll go to the circus right away," Arwyn told him.

"See that you do, I want this man found and brought back to the city before the New Year," Captain Jonnes Smith barked and quickly left the police house.

It didn't bother Arwyn that the visit had been a brief one; being around his superior officer always made him feel very uncomfortable.

He didn't wait for the chief constable's carriage to depart before he had his cloak around his shoulders and was making his way out to the circus camp.

Arwyn marched through the snow. He debated going via the lodge and asking Mr Hunter to accompany him, but considering how much the chief constable disliked Alex, Arwyn decided it was best not to involve him in official police business.

The same two women as before were stood outside the camp, still doing laundry. The moment Constable Evans came into view, they dropped their washing and disappeared inside the nearest tent.

A few minutes later, the same three men as last time marched out of the camp to bar the way into the camp.

"Constable, how can we help you?" Bairstow asked when Arwyn was still some distance away.

"I'm looking for a man by the name of Paul Curran," Constable Evans said as loudly as he could.

"There's no one by that name here," Bairstow shrugged.

"I'm sure that I can trust you to be a man of your word, but I need to search your camp. He could be using a false name or hiding in an odd corner of your camp," Arwyn replied as he tried to walk past the three men.

"You won't find anyone here that doesn't belong, and Bairstow already told you that there is no one here by the name of Paul Curran," the giant man said firmly.

"Easy now, Dominic," Bairstow warned.

"Are you telling me that I can't search your camp?" Arwyn asked as he glared up at the man-mountain.

"There is no one here called Paul Curran. We have performances to get ready for, so you'll have to leave," the small man said in an even voice.

Arwyn looked between the three men and wished he'd gone to fetch Mr Hunter.

He slowly backed away from the circus camp without saying a word, formulating a plan as he went.

Chapter 10

Cooky had recovered from the shock of the children trying to break into the henhouse. It had been a few days since it had happened, and during those days one of the maids had been sent out to feed the hens instead of the cook.

But with the change of atmosphere in Grangeback, Cooky was glad of the chance to be outside with her beloved chickens.

She was humming happily to herself as she stepped out into the cold air, carrying a basin of chicken feed under her arm.

She waddled down the path and undid the latch on the henhouse and began to scatter the seed. She bustled between the birds, checking the fencing for any signs of holes or digging around the edge.

Cooky was about to return to the house, satisfied that there was nothing wrong when a cough came from inside the wooden structure at the centre of the coop.

The cook froze and slowly cast her eyes at the

henhouse. She was shaking slightly, hoping that the cough had just been her very limited imagination, but then there was a second cough.

She didn't know what to do. Her heart was pounding with sheer terror. She cast her eyes around looking for help to come from somewhere.

From around the side of the house, a shower of powder was kicked, announcing the arrival of Pattinson.

The Japanese hunting dog loved jumping in the snow, no matter how long he was out in soft, white wonderland.

"Mr Hunter, are you there?" Cooky called out tentatively.

Pattinson heard the cook's voice and went bounding towards the hen house. As he drew closer, the animal suddenly started growling.

"Pattinson, what are you doing?" Alex asked as he appeared and laid his hand on the dog's neck, "Cooky, what are you doing?" he frowned as he noticed the cook standing perfectly still in the coop.

"Oh! Mr Hunter! Someone is coughing in the henhouse," Cooky wailed. Pattinson was still growling.

"Stay," Mr Hunter ordered the dog as he undid the

latch and went in to rescue Cooky.

The hunter made his way over to the hen house and opened the door that let the cook collect the eggs the hens laid.

It took a moment for his eyes to adjust to the darkness, but as they did, he could see that there wasn't anything out of place. He was beginning to think it was simply Cooky's paranoia that had led her to hear coughing when he heard it himself.

It was coming from underneath the lowest row of nests. Alex got down on his hands and knees and found himself face to face with a stocky man who had dark hair but was clean-shaven.

"Come out from under there," Alex said firmly, getting to his feet and giving the man plenty of room to crawl out from under the nests.

The man slowly made his way out from under the nests, coughing to clear his lungs of all the dust and dirt that he had been breathing in.

"Who are you?" Mr Hunter asked as the man knelt on the floor in front of him.

"My name is Paul Curran, please I'm sorry for hiding here, but there was nowhere else," the man spluttered.

"Why are you hiding?" Alex asked.

"Please, I haven't had anything to eat for days," Paul begged.

"You can't stay here, come with me," Mr Hunter replied.

"Where are you taking me?" the man looked terrified.

"To the lodge. You can have something to eat and drink and tell me what is going on," Alex said, his voice was softer than it had been.

Paul looked at him with searching eyes. He wasn't sure whether he could trust the man that was stood over him, but at this moment he wasn't left with many options.

He nodded meekly, and shakily rose to his feet. Cooky had managed to move so that she was stood outside the wire of the coop when Alex led Paul Curran out of the henhouse.

Pattinson had stopped growling and was sat quite placidly next to the cook.

"Oh! Mr Hunter! I will never be able to come near my hens again!" Cooky declared as she looked at the man that was following Alex.

"Calm down, Cooky, there's nothing to be afraid of. Your chickens are all safe. Don't mention this to anyone though; I will sort it all out," Alex said gently.

"Oh! Mr Hunter! You are so brave. I promise I won't tell a soul," Cooky promised.

Alex smiled at her as he walked past. Pattinson fell into step beside his master. The men walked in silence across the estate. Every few steps Paul would trip, and Alex would have to help him back to his feet, but they eventually made it to the lodge.

Mr Hunter built a fire and sat Paul down in front of it whilst he made something for the man to eat. When he had been fed and given tea to drink, Alex spoke.

"Why were you hiding in the hen house?" the hunter asked.

"I made a mistake in Chester. I got into a fight with some men. They were drunk, and so I won easily, but they went to the police, and now I have to hide from them," Paul said glumly.

"You got into a fight?" Alex asked with a raised eyebrow.

"I was walking down the street, and these men attacked me. I hadn't done anything to provoke them. They just saw me and then attacked me," Paul replied earnestly.

"But you fought back?" Alex continued.

"I wasn't going to let them just beat me until someone came along," Paul replied.

"I see, and they went to the police?" Alex sighed.

"One of them ran off when I started fighting back and came running over with a pair of policemen. I had to run away," Paul whined.

"How long have you been in the hen house?" Alex asked.

"Since Christmas Eve. The children from the circus I belong to were bringing me food and water, but they stopped. I think they got caught by that cook. I heard her screaming," Paul said.

"That explains the story the ringmaster and his friends told us," Mr Hunter said, shaking his head.

"We thought that the police might come and try to search the circus camp, but they wouldn't think of looking for me in the hen house of one of the great houses," Paul explained.

"No, I don't suppose they would. You can sleep here tonight. I will have to think about what to do," Alex rubbed his eyes and went upstairs to sort out a bed for his house guest.

Why can't life ever be as simple as hunting in the woods? He thought as he climbed the stairs.

Chapter 11

Cooky was good at many things, but one thing that she truly was terrible at is keeping a secret. So when Constable Evans came to Grangeback to ask whether anyone had seen any sign of the man he was looking for, she told him everything almost instantly.

Arwyn had set off for the lodge just as the snow started to fall. It came down in light flurries that steadily got heavier until Arwyn couldn't see his hand in front of his face.

The snowdrifts got harder to negotiate as they grew higher. Where they had been halfway up the constable's calf before the snow started to fall, they now reached his waist.

Rather than stepping through the white powder, he was now wading, struggling against the weather. There were times that he wasn't sure that he was even going in the right direction.

It wasn't until he finally managed to reach the trees and gained some shelter from the snow that he discovered that he was half a mile to the south of where he had intended to be.

By the time that Arwyn reached the lodge, he was colder than he had ever been in his life and in great need of a fire.

He walked round to the back of the lodge and tried the back door. It was commonly known around Stickleback Hollow that Mr Hunter didn't lock the back door of the lodge and that anyone who wanted to see him was welcome to walk in.

When Arwyn tried the handle, it wouldn't turn, and when he pushed against the door, he found that it was locked.

"Hunter!" Constable Evans hammered on the door. The sound of movement came from inside the lodge, "Hunter! Open the door. It's Arwyn."

"I'm afraid I can't let you in," Alex shouted his reply.

"Don't be a fool; there's a blizzard out here!" Arwyn shouted back.

"And what brings you to my door in a blizzard?" Mr Hunter asked.

"Paul Curran," Constable Evans sighed.

"That's why I can't let you in," Alex replied.

"Hunter, I know you're a good man, but I need to

106

arrest him. The Chief Constable came to tell me to bring him to Chester. Cooky told me you brought him here. Captain Jonnes Smith won't look too kindly on you sheltering the man he is looking for," Arwyn called back.

"Do what you have to do, Constable Evans, and I will do what I have to," Mr Hunter replied.

Arwyn kicked the snow with frustration and stood trying to think as the cold seeped even deeper into his bones.

The sound of a carriage coming down the road was barely audible over the wind. Arwyn marched through the trees until he found the road and recognised the carriage as one that belonged to Grangeback.

The driver stopped the carriage when he saw the policeman coming through the trees.

"What's going on?" Grace asked from the depths of the carriage.

"It's Constable Evans!" the driver replied. Grace stuck her head out of the window and beckoned for the constable to join her.

"Miss Read, where's Lady Sarah?" Arwyn asked at the carriage window. He was shivering so much that the words barely escaped his chattering teeth.

"She was in Stickleback Hollow, but that was hours ago, I expect she is back at the house now. Arwyn, please get in, your almost frozen solid," Grace said kindly.

Constable Evans was only too glad to climb into the carriage out of the terrible weather.

"Take us to Grangeback," Grace called to the driver, and the carriage lurched off.

By the time the carriage reached the house, the horses and driver were all in need of thawing. Grace hurried the constable into the house and took him to the dining room. The largest fireplace in the house was in the dining room, and it was kept lit from the time the servants first awoke until they went to bed.

She placed the constable and went in search of Lady Sarah. Lady Sarah was in the library, scrawling something on writing paper when Grace found her.

"How was Millie when you left her?" Sarah asked.

"Much calmer, but still upset," Grace replied.

"Very understandably. You should get to bed, Grace, you don't look well at all," Lady Sarah said with a measure of concern.

"I will. Constable Evans is waiting for you in the dining

room. He was out in the blizzard. We found him on the road near the lodge," Grace explained.

"Thank you, Grace, rest well," Sarah said as a flicker of a frown passed over her face. When she was sure that Grace had started climbing the stairs to her room, Sarah made her way to the dining room.

Arwyn had taken off his cloak and had draped it over the back of a chair to dry. He was still shivering, but he had started to regain the feeling in his hands and feet.

"Constable Evans, what brings you out in such inclement weather?" Sarah asked as she entered the dining room.

"It's something of a long story," Arwyn replied. He related the events of the day to Sarah from the arrival of Captain Jonnes Smith to the being denied entry to the lodge.

"I see, so why have you come to me?" Sarah asked.

"Because if you go and talk to Hunter, he will listen to you. If you tell him that he needs to hand Paul Curran over to me so that the police can deal with what happened, then he will. It's in his best interest to not get involved," Arwyn explained.

"I see. When does the chief constable expect you to

have resolved all of this?" Sarah asked.

"Before midnight tomorrow," Constable Evans replied.

"I make no promises, but I will go talk to Mr Hunter," Sarah sighed.

"Thank you, I'll make my way back to the village then," Arwyn smiled.

"Don't be a fool. The blizzard is still raging, and you're frozen stiff. I'll have Mrs Bosworth prepare a room for you. You can stay tonight and go back in the morning," Sarah said firmly and went off in search of Mrs Bosworth before Constable Evans could refuse.

Chapter 12

The blizzard lasted throughout the night, but by the morning, the world around Grangeback was still and quiet.

The pristine snow glistened under the rays of the rising sun and made for almost perfect riding conditions as far as Sarah was concerned.

The visit to Stickleback Hollow the previous day had left Grace in a rather desperate state, and no amount of arguing could prevent Mrs Bosworth from locking Grace in her room.

Sarah dressed and made her way down to the stables without Grace in tow. She had promised that she would go and speak to Alex about Paul Curran, but she needed to go and visit the circus first.

Black Guy was anxious to be let out of his stable after several days of being cooped up in it. The pair set off through the freshly fallen snow and across the land of Grangeback to the circus camp on the lands of Duffleton.

As Sarah approached the camp, only one of the women

left to fetch the men in the tent. Rather than coming out to meet Sarah, as they had for Arwyn and Alex, they waited for her at the edge of the camp.

"Good morning, milady. What brings you out to our camp in such weather?" Bairstow asked as Sarah brought Black Guy to a halt by the three men.

"I came to talk to the ringmaster; I assume that is you," Sarah said as she looked down at the three men.

"I am. The name is Bairstow. Who are you?" the ringmaster said as Sarah dismounted.

"I am Lady Montgomery Baird Watson-Wentworth from the Grangeback estate," Sarah introduced herself as her feet touched the ground.

"A pleasure, milady. May I introduce Mr Dominic Smith and Mr Peter Libby," Bairstow pointed to the giant man first and then to the smaller one.

"Gentleman, can one of you take care of my horse whilst I talk with Mr Bairstow?" Sarah asked with a smile.

"It would be an honour," Peter bowed slightly and took Black Guy's reins from Sarah.

Bairstow led the lady into the tent that the three men had emerged from, and Dominic remained outside to make sure that nobody went in uninvited.

"So what business is it that you wish to talk about? Missing property or Mr Paul Curran," Bairstow asked as the pair sat down.

The tent was filled with a range of costumes and boxes. A table had been made out of two barrels and a plank of wood. Sarah sat on a chest on one side of the table whilst Bairstow sat on the other.

"I have no need to ask about Mr Curran. I know where he is, and he is safe for the moment," Sarah replied. A look of panic briefly flickered over the ringmaster's face, "I came to talk to you about the missing property. All the items are small and mostly worth very little. This suggests that the thief isn't someone that is trying to profit from the theft."

"What are you saying?" Bairstow frowned.

"I think you know who the thief is and you are trying to protect them as best you can. Constable Evans doesn't believe that anything has been stolen, that the property has simply been lost. There will be no trouble from the police if the items are simply returned," Sarah replied.

"Dominic, go fetch Emily," Bairstow shouted.

"She really doesn't mean anything about it. She can't

help herself. We try to make sure that she is never on her own, but she was so excited about seeing her sister that she has been running off in search of her since we arrived. When we heard people talking about things going missing, we made sure that she didn't leave the camp, but the damage had already been done," Bairstow sighed.

"Her sister?" Sarah asked.

"Yes, Grace Read," Bairstow replied, and Sarah laughed.

"I'm sorry, Grace is my maid. She has been helping me talk to the people that Emily stole from. She would be with me now; only she has been forced to stay in bed with a terrible cold," Sarah explained. The flap of the tent was pushed aside a petit blonde girl scurried in.

"Emily, this is the lady that your sister works for. She has come to take back all the things that you have stolen," Bairstow told the girl in a matter-of-fact tone.

"Am I in trouble?" Emily asked. She was a few years younger than Grace, but she was the spitting image of her sister.

"No, if you give me back everything that was taken, then I will make sure that it is returned and that will be the end of it," Sarah assured her.

"I'll go and fetch the things," Emily said. She disappeared out of the tent.

"Can I ask, where is Paul?" Bairstow enquired nervously.

"I believe he is at the lodge on the Grangeback estate. The cook found him in the hen house, and the gamekeeper took him to the lodge and kept him from the constable," Sarah said. Relief flooded over the face of the ringmaster.

"We were hoping to hide him until we moved on; he isn't the kind of man to cause trouble or to get involved with fights," Bairstow said earnestly.

"If Mr Hunter is protecting him, then he has a good reason to," Sarah soothed.

Emily returned to the tent carrying an armful of assorted items and handed them over to Sarah.

Sarah didn't spend long in the circus camp; it wasn't even lunchtime when she arrived at the lodge and knocked on the front door.

"I'm still not letting you in, Arwyn," Alex shouted from somewhere inside the house.

"It's not Arwyn," Sarah replied. The bolt on the door

was pulled back, and Mr Hunter opened the door.

"Arwyn told me what happened yesterday," Sarah said.

"Are you here to tell me to hand Paul over to the police?" Alex asked.

"I'm here to listen to why," Sarah replied.

"Then you better come in," Alex sighed.

Chapter 18

Constable Evans left Grangeback before breakfast was served. He already felt uncomfortable enough about staying the night in the manor house; staying for breakfast would have almost been unbearable.

He resisted the temptation to go back to the lodge and try to reason with Alex through the door and instead made his way back to the village.

He decided it was best if he returned to the police house to wait for news from Lady Sarah about how her discussion with Mr Hunter had gone.

The constable was rather restless on the walk back to the police house and even more so when he finally reached his home. He paced up and down the hallway, glancing at the clock above the fire every few minutes.

Time seemed to be going by incredibly slowly, and at one point Arwyn was convinced that the hands of the clock had turned backwards.

He was on the verge of going out in search of Sarah

when there was a knock at the door. Arwyn threw it open and was rewarded with the sight of Lady Sarah stood holding a saddlebag in her hand.

"What is in there?" the constable asked as Sarah handed it to him and walked into the sitting room.

"Mr Claydon's pocket knife, Reverend Butterfield's brass candlestick, Mr Christian's worn out brass boot, Miss Gunn's silver fork, Wilson's pewter tankard and Miss Roy's pearl broach," Sarah replied with a smile as she sat down.

"You found all of that?" Arwyn asked in surprise as he opened the saddlebags and slowly emptied the contents out onto the side table.

"I did," Sarah replied.

"Where was it?" the constable looked at Sarah suspiciously.

"That's not important. The items have all been found and returned." Sarah assured Arwyn.

"What about the fishing rod and the leather tools?" Constable Evans asked.

"They weren't there," her ladyship replied.

"Are you sure that they weren't there?" Arwyn frowned.

118

"Positive and nothing else will go missing by the same method from now on," Sarah said firmly.

"Then where are the fishing rod and leather tools?" Constable Evans asked crossly.

"I don't know, but they are useful items, most of these are sentimental trinkets," Sarah shrugged.

"Whoever took them had a use for them then," Arwyn said slowly.

"It makes sense, though who would need a fishing rod and leather tools, aside for someone like Mr Hunter?" Sarah asked.

"No one, do you think that Duffleton's new gamekeeper is responsible for the thefts?" Arwyn clasped his hands behind his back as he thought.

"I haven't met him, and Mr Hunter hasn't mentioned anything about him," Sarah replied.

"I haven't met him either. I will try and find out what I can about him before I go to Duffleton to talk to him," Arwyn sighed.

"It would be wise to consider that someone else could have stolen the items. A vagrant or a traveller that is living off the land could also have stolen them," Sarah suggested.

"What do I do with these things now?" Arwyn asked.

"Take them back to their owners. Tell them they have been recovered. Mr Christian might ask who took his boot in the first place, he has a rather fertile imagination, but the others will simply be pleased to have their property back," Sarah replied.

"And what do I tell Mr Christian?" Arwyn asked.

"Tell him you found it in a pawn shop in Chester. He won't know it's not true and it will stop his stories," Sarah smiled.

"Thank you for finding these things. I'm sorry for what I said to you at the inn, your ladyship," Arwyn said uncomfortably.

"I should have been more tactful when I went to talk to people about these items, it was my fault," Sarah replied apologetically.

"Thank you, my lady. Did you go to talk to Mr Hunter this morning?" the constable asked, changing the subject.

"I did," Sarah said with a sigh.

"And?" Arwyn asked expectantly.

"If the chief constable really wants to arrest that man, then he will have to go through Mr Hunter to do it," Sarah

120

replied.

"Captain Jonnes Smith already hates Hunter; he would have no qualms about throwing him into jail, right beside Paul Curran. He knows that he can't interfere like this and not escape unscathed," Arwyn railed.

"He dislikes injustice. He takes a stand for those he believes are being oppressed. No amount of threatening will dissuade him from protecting this man," Sarah replied calmly.

"I know that Hunter is a stubborn man, but I thought that he would listen to you if you told him to let this go," Arwyn said as he walked over to the fire and slammed his fist on the mantelpiece.

"I didn't tell him to stand aside," Sarah said as she rose from her seat, "I know that you have a job that you have to do, and I don't want to see Mr Hunter thrown into jail, but I won't be the one to tell him that he has to sacrifice his principles for my sake or to save his own skin. If I were you, I would return the broach to Miss Roy first and finish with returning the pocket knife to Mr Christian."

Arwyn watched the lady leave and shook his head. It was not going to be a pleasant end to the year for the constable. He looked at the items on the table and decided that he would send one of the Baker boys to Chester to tell the chief constable what was happening with Paul Curran. Then he would return the missing property.

Whatever was going to happen in Stickleback Hollow before the close of the year, Arwyn knew that he was going to be very lonely at the start of the new one.

Chapter 14

Stanley Baker came back from Chester with Chief Constable Captain Jonnes Smith, Constable Cantello, Constable McIntyre, Constable Meyers, Constable Clowes, Constable Kelly and Constable McGill.

The assembled constabulary arrived at the police house, just as Constable Evans returned from returning the missing items to their owners.

"The boy said you have news about this Paul Curran character," Captain Jonnes Smith greeted Arwyn.

"Yes, sir, he is in the area, and he does belong to the circus. The performers are all acting suspiciously and refused to allow me into the camp to search for him," Constable Evans replied with a sharp salute.

Though Arwyn knew that the chief constable would find out that Mr Hunter was hiding Paul Curran in his lodge eventually, but he had decided that he wasn't going to be the one to betray his friend.

The constable had already had to arrest Mr Hunter

once this year. At the time, Alex hadn't been the most popular person in Stickleback Hollow, but Lady Sarah had made the hunter much more amiable since then. Constable Evans was convinced that if he had to arrest Alex a second time, the reaction of the citizenry of Stickleback Hollow would be somewhat adverse to his health.

"Men, Constable Evans will take us to the circus camp. We will search it for this Paul Curran. You all know what he looks like and you all know how dangerous he is," Captain Jonnes Smith instructed the men he had brought from Chester.

The policemen had arrived in a cart driven by four horses. They piled into the back of the cart with the chief constable sitting up front with Arwyn as he drove the cart.

With the snow on the ground and very little traffic using the road between Duffleton Hall and the village of Stickleback Hollow, it took much longer than it would have ordinarily have done to reach the site of the circus camp.

It seemed that all of the performers in the circus had turned out to stand in a line between the camp and the police force.

"Here we go," Constable Clowes whispered as the policemen climbed out of the cart.

124

"Can we help you?" Bairstow asked from the edge of the camp.

"I am Captain Jonnes Smith, chief constable of the Cheshire Constabulary. My officers are here to search your camp for the wanted criminal, Paul Curran," the chief constable shouted his reply.

"And what if we refuse to let your officers into our camp?" Dominic called back.

"Then you will all be arrested for attempting to pervert the course of justice," Captain Jonnes Smith said sternly.

The circus performers muttered to one another for a few minutes whilst the policemen slowly walked towards them.

As the policemen reached the line around the camp, the circus performers stood to one side and allowed the policemen to pass.

"Follow them," Bairstow hissed to Dominic, "Make sure that Matthew keeps Emily out of sight," he said, turning to Peter.

The two men went to do what the ringmaster had said. Bairstow returned to his tent and sat at his makeshift table.

He knew that the policemen weren't going to find Paul

in the circus camp, but he was worried about what they would threaten to do if Paul didn't give himself up.

After a few minutes of deciding what should be done, Bairstow went in search of the circus clown.

"Toby, I need to go to the house on the Grangeback estate. Ask the Lady Sarah where the lodge is. Tell Paul he needs to give himself up. We'll get everything straightened out, but the chief constable is here, and that's not a good sign," Bairstow instructed. Toby nodded and ran off through the snow.

The police searched the camp for an hour but found no sign of Paul Curran. They were all cold, dejected and longing to be sat in the warmth of an inn.

"Paul Curran has until the end of today to give himself up. If he doesn't, then we'll arrest everyone who belongs to the circus and hold you until he comes in," Captain Jonnes Smith told Bairstow in no uncertain terms.

Bairstow knew that there was nothing he could do except nod and watch the policemen piling back into the cart.

"What do we do?" Dominic asked Bairstow as the two men stood watching the cart drive back towards Stickleback Hollow.

"It's already been done. Sooner or later, someone will tell them where Paul is hiding, he needs to give himself up and make it all easier on himself," Bairstow sighed and shook his head.

"You know that he didn't start any fight in Chester," Peter said as he joined them.

"I know, but I need to think about what is best for the circus as a whole, not just one man," Bairstow replied.

Chapter 15

Toby Craggs may have been a clown, but he was one of the fastest runners that Bairstow had ever known. Whenever he needed someone to take urgent messages, it was Toby that he called on.

Even in the snow, he was surprisingly quick and very difficult to follow. Even if the police had spotted Toby leaving the circus camp, they wouldn't have been able to keep up with him.

It didn't take long for him to reach Grangeback and ask for directions to the lodge. Cooky had been terrified by the sight of a man running towards the house and had told everyone that would listen, she wasn't going outside again until the circus had gone.

Mrs Bosworth had taken Cooky away to calm her down whilst Lady Sarah dealt with the visitor.

"I'm sorry to disturb you, mum, but I need to know how to get to the lodge," Toby mumbled as he stood in the hallway of Grangeback.

Sarah decided that it would be best to take Toby to the lodge rather than send him with vague directions. She doubted that Mr Hunter would open the door to the circus performer if he went without an escort.

"Who is it?" Alex called out when Sarah knocked on the door of the lodge.

"It's me. I have a messenger from the circus. Bairstow sent him," Sarah replied. Mr Hunter opened the door and ushered the pair into his home.

"Toby?" Paul asked as he stood on the stairs.

"Paul! Bairstow says you need to go to the police and give yourself up," Toby said as he rushed over to his friend.

"What? Are you mad?" Paul demanded.

"The police, they came to the camp. They're going to arrest everyone if you don't turn yourself in," Toby explained desperately.

"They can't do that!" Paul cried.

"Yes, they can, and they'll keep everyone in jail until you turn yourself in," Toby said sadly.

"And if you stay here, they'll find you; arrest you, everyone in the circus and Mr Hunter," Sarah added.

"But I didn't do anything wrong!" Paul moaned.

"If that's really true, then you won't be in jail forever, just until the truth comes out," Sarah said, trying her best to be encouraging.

"If the truth comes out," Alex said dryly.

"What am I going to do?" Paul asked as he collapsed onto the bottom step with his head in his hands.

"There may be someone who can help," Alex replied slowly, "Sarah, can you stay here and watch over these two until I get back?" he asked.

"Of course, where are you going?" Sarah frowned slightly as she spoke.

"I won't be long," was all the reply she received. Mr Hunter made his way across the estate. He strode with purpose, though he wasn't entirely sure what he was going to do when he reached his destination.

George was sat in the drawing room when Alex strode through the French windows.

"Alex, what are you doing here? Sarah is out at the moment," George began as he looked at his son. In truth, he hadn't expected to see Mr Hunter for quite some time, especially when he had left in such an abrupt manner before.

"I came to see you. There's something I need your help

with," Mr Hunter replied curtly. He was still unsure how he felt about the brigadier. Discovering that George was his father brought an overwhelming number of questions to mind, most of which the young hunter hadn't even begun to process.

"Anything you need is yours," George said solemnly.

Alex took a deep breath and began to explain to the situation that Paul Curran was in. George listened without saying a word, and when Mr Hunter had finished, he thought for a few minutes before he opened his mouth to speak.

"You think that this man won't be treated fairly if Captain Jonnes Smith arrests him?" George asked.

"I don't think any man that travels from place to place is ever treated fairly by the people that live in a town or city where he is suspected of committing a crime," Alex replied.

"I see your point, but surely there are witnesses who can bear out an account of events to support one party or the other," George frowned.

"From what Paul said, there is no one. It will be one man's word against the other," Alex sighed.

"And the man who travels from place to place will be the one to suffer," George concluded.

"Is there anything that can be done to help him?" Mr Hunter asked.

"I'll take him to the Reverend Butterfield. He can seek sanctuary in the church; it's not something that Captain Jonnes Smith will dare to violate," George replied.

"Sanctuary was abolished," Alex said, shaking his head.

"I'm glad to see you were paying attention in school, but just because the king abolished it in law doesn't mean that the church doesn't protect those who need it. Abolitionists and slaves around the world are protected by sanctuary when they seek it, and Reverend Butterfield is very well respected. If Captain Jonnes Smith tried to take this Paul Curran out of the church by force, he would be facing the wrath of some very powerful men, and the one who is greater than us all," George said with as much reassurance as he could muster.

"I'll go and fetch him from the lodge," Alex replied and turned to leave.

"No, I'll come to the lodge with the carriage, he won't be seen by anyone that might happen to visit the house," George stood up and walked towards the door of the drawing room to order the carriage.

"I'll go ahead of you," Mr Hunter grunted as he made his way towards the French windows.

"There's no need, come with me in the carriage," the brigadier insisted.

"No, thank you. I prefer to walk," Alex shot back.

"I'm glad that you came to me for help, my boy, but do you ever think that you will be able to forgive me?" George asked sadly.

"I don't know," Mr Hunter replied and stepped back out into the cold.

Chapter 16

Alex arrived back at the lodge only a few minutes before George arrived with the carriage. Grace was with George when the carriage arrived.

"Mr Curran, we're going to take you to the church where the Reverend will take care of you. Grace is going to stay with you to ensure that if you need anything, or anything happens, we can be informed at once," the brigadier explained as they bundled Paul into the carriage.

"Thank you, for all your help," Paul said as he leaned out of the window of the carriage before it lurched off in the direction of the church. Toby had already set off at a run to take the news back to the circus about Paul.

"We need to go to Chester and find out what really happened in that fight," Alex said as he and Sarah stood watching the carriage disappear.

Pattinson had padded out into the snow and butted his head against Mr Hunter's leg.

"The chief constable won't be happy," Sarah replied.

"No, I don't suppose he will be, but it's only a matter of time before he finds out where Paul is being hidden, and the people of Bairstow's circus are going to suffer if we can't find out the truth," Alex said as he reached down and scratched Pattinson behind the ears.

"Then we should go fetch the horses," Sarah smiled and planted a fleeting kiss on his cheek as she moved past him.

The weather was clear as the pair rode into the city with Pattinson trotting along beside them, Sarah leading the way. The streets were surprisingly busy given the cold weather, but even so, it didn't take them long to reach the Blossoms hotel on St. John's Street.

With the New Year fast approaching, there was an excited feel to the city, and the atmosphere inside the hotel was far more intense than then last time the pair had been there.

The clerk behind the desk looked up as Sarah made her way over.

"Your ladyship, a pleasure to have you with us again, and your escort is here as well. Can I assume that you require a room for the night, the royal suite again, perhaps?" the clerk oiled as Sarah looked down at him.

"Yes, the royal suite will be fine, and my dog will also be staying. See that the kitchen prepares something suitable for him," Sarah said with a wave of her hand. Alex had to suppress his desire to laugh as he watched the clerk attempting to ingratiate himself to the young lady, whilst Sarah played the part of a spoilt lady of society.

"I wonder what he would think if he knew why we were here in the city," Alex mused as the door to the room was shut behind them.

"He wouldn't believe that a lady would ever associate with such individuals as Mr Curran, let alone search for a man on his behalf," Sarah smiled.

"I suppose not. We should go to the Mitre Inn on Pepper Street and speak to William, if anyone has heard anything about this incident, William will have," Mr Hunter stood leaning on the wall by the door to the room. Sarah nodded and followed Alex out of the hotel.

Pattinson padded along next to Sarah as they walked down the streets of the Roman city. The horses had been stabled at the hotel, and it wasn't a long way to walk from St. John's Street to Pepper Street.

The Mitre Inn was not the kind of establishment that a

lady of Sarah's standing would normally frequent, but it was one of the best places to get information.

William Lloyd was the owner and the man that stood watch over the city of Chester from behind the bar. Mr Hunter had known him for a number of years, and the two of them were friendly.

"Hunter, it's been a while, and you've brought your friend again. A pleasure to see you both. What can I do for you?" Mr Lloyd asked from behind the bar at the back of the inn.

"We were wondering if you heard anything about a fight that happened before Christmas," Alex said as he pushed through the crowd of people to reach William.

"Lots of fights happen every day around here, you know that," Mr Lloyd replied with a wry smile.

"We're interested in the fight that has Paul Curran being hunted by the police," Sarah said as she followed Alex. Pattinson stuck close to Sarah's side and growled at a few of the men that he considered to be a threat to the woman he guarded.

"Ah, that fight. Well, that was an interesting one, but nothing I can tell you about it," William shrugged.

"I see, well, can't be helped, I guess," Alex replied, gently taking Sarah by the arm and moving her so that she was positioned behind him.

Before Sarah knew what was happening, a stool had been broken on the bar, and a man was trying to hit Alex around the head with one of the broken legs.

Pattinson leapt at the man and clamped his powerful jaws around the man's arm. He cried out in pain and dropped the chair leg. The dog dragged him to the floor as a second man tried to lunge at Mr Hunter.

Alex waited until the second man was a foot away from him before he knocked him to one side with his giant fist.

Sarah was backed into a corner, completely protected by the hunter's frame. She couldn't see what was going on, but she could hear the sound of the fight, and in her mind, it was far worse than it actually was.

There were only four men, and all of them were much smaller and weaker than Mr Hunter was. None of them had fought a man like Alex before, and none of them had ever seen a dog like Pattinson.

With the dog fighting one man, Mr Hunter dispatched the other three with a minimal amount of effort. When the four of the men lying on the floor of the inn, and in no condition to continue fighting, Alex let Sarah out of the corner and turned to William.

"The men that were fighting with Paul?" Mr Hunter asked.

"The men that attacked Paul," William confirmed.

"Any idea why they did?" Alex asked.

"There was a girl called Emily that the men tried to take. Mr Curran stopped them. Not sure why. The men were saying that the girl had stolen something from them," Mr Lloyd shrugged.

"That makes sense," Sarah sighed as she stepped over the fallen men. Pattinson sat, wagging his tail, looking as innocent as a dog with a muzzle that was wet with blood could.

"Is that why he won't turn himself in to the police? Because of this girl?" Alex asked Sarah.

"Yes, I will tell you about it on the way back to Stickleback Hollow. We should take these men and tell the chief constable what really happen," Sarah said as she looked down on the groaning men.

"He's not going to be happy we've interfered again,"

Alex grinned.

"No, but I think he will be even less happy that these men lied to him and caused such a problem when he should be at home preparing for the New Year," Sarah smiled.

Chapter 17

The Reverend Percy Butterfield was only too pleased to grant Paul sanctuary after George explained the situation.

The reverend showed Paul and Grace to the clock room in the bell tower. It was a room that was out of the way and quite a climb up some very steep, rickety stairs.

There was no furniture in the room, but the reverend brought up some blankets and sacks stuffed with straw to make the clock room more comfortable.

Paul sat on the floor whilst Grace looked at the clock machinery that took up part of the room.

"Why did you agree to come and keep me company?" Paul asked after the pair had been sat in silence for more than half an hour.

"I used to be part of the Bairstow Circus. My parents were part of it, my brother and sister still are. I left because I didn't have any talent for circus life," Grace said as she ran her hands over the glass of the clock face.

"What do you do now?" Paul asked.

"I'm a lady's maid at Grangeback," Grace smiled.

"You're the maid for the girl that came to the lodge?" Paul looked over at Grace with a funny expression on his face.

"Her name is Lady Montgomery Baird Watson-Wentworth. She's not what you might expect, but she is a good woman. She's very kind, and she and Mr Hunter will do whatever they can to help you," Grace replied shortly.

"They've both given me more help than I would have expected of country folk. Have you spoken to your brother or your sister recently?" Paul pulled his knees to his chest and hugged them tightly.

"No, not for a few years now, why do you ask?" Grace frowned.

"Emily, well, she's not quite right. There's something wrong with her mind. She keeps taking things from people. It started a few years ago, just after your parents died. Matthew's been doing his best to keep her out of trouble, and everyone helps, but sometimes -"

"Is she unhappy?" Grace asked, spinning around to look at Paul.

"Sometimes. The men I was fighting, they said she took something from them and tried to take her away," Paul rested his chin on his knees.

"You fought them to save Emily?" asked Grace.

"I just told them to leave her alone, and they attacked me," Paul shrugged.

"Is she alright?" Grace asked.

"Matthew got her back to the circus. I don't know what happened after they left Chester. You'd be better talking to your brother," Paul replied.

"I'm not sure that he will be keen to talk to me. He wasn't happy when I left the circus to do something else," Grace sighed.

"You haven't spoken to him since you left?" Paul sounded surprised.

"No, we haven't written or spoken to one another for years," Grace said sadly.

"Maybe this would be a good time for you to go see him," Paul suggested.

"Maybe, but not until this has been resolved," Grace replied.

The reverend was bustling around the church below, making sure that everything was where it should be before he went to prepare some food for his guests.

"Good evening, reverend," Arwyn's voice echoed through the church.

"Constable Evans, what a pleasure to see you. Can I offer you some tea and cake? Mrs Mullaney brought the most delicious Christmas cake round earlier, and I would be delighted to share it with you," Reverend Butterfield beamed at the young policeman.

"I'm afraid that I am not here for tea and cake, reverend. I am looking for a man called Paul Curran," Arwyn replied seriously.

"Well, that is disappointing, it has been a while since we last spoke and I do want to talk to you about the next cricket season. I think we need to find a left-arm fast swing bowler to balance the Stickleback Hollow team," the reverend replied with a slightly glazed look in his eye.

"Reverend, this is not the time to discuss our bowling line up. I know that we need a new bowler after Doctor Hales told us that he won't be playing any more, but I need to know about Paul Curran. Is he here?" Arwyn sounded exasperated.

"He is. It's such a shame about Doctor Hales. He was such a good seam bowler, but with the teams that we will be playing against this next season, I am certain we need someone who can put some more pace on the ball," the reverend continued.

"Reverend, please, tell me where Paul Curran is. I am here to arrest him," Arwyn said, trying to control his frustration.

"Oh, you can't do that; the church has granted him sanctuary," the reverend said with a wave of his hand, "now, I was thinking, that maybe we can persuade Mr Hunter to bowl."

"The church has granted him sanctuary?" Arwyn half-groaned.

"Yes, of course it has. Rumour has it that Mr Hunter was an excellent bowler in his school days, absolutely hopeless with a bat, but we have Mr Moore who can more than compensate for that," the reverend kept talking, seemingly oblivious to Constable Evans reaction.

Arwyn didn't even bid the reverend a good day as he turned away and walked out of the church. Outside, Captain Jonnes Smith was waiting for news. They had gone to Stickleback Hollow and asked the villagers if they had seen anyone. It had been Lee Baker suggesting that anyone trying to hide from the police would be at the church that had turned the constabulary's attention to the house of worship.

"Well?" the chief constable asked.

"Paul Curran has been granted sanctuary," Arwyn replied.

"Surround the church," Captain Jonnes Smith ordered that six policemen that stood with him, "we may not be able to go into the church and arrest him, but the moment he leaves the church, we can arrest him. No one can stay cooped up in a church forever."

"Yes, sir," the policemen chorused.

Chapter 18

It was a cold day for the police to spend standing around a church, especially when it was New Year's Eve. The longer they spent waiting, the terser the chief constable became.

By the time that Sarah and Alex returned from Chester, it was already 8 o'clock, and no one at the church was in good spirits.

"Good evening, Chief Constable," Sarah called out as they arrived. The pair were riding on Harald and Black Guy. Behind them a cart was being driven by a young man from the Mitre Inn. The cart contained the four men that had attacked Mr Hunter in the bar. All of them looked worse for wear and had their hands tied behind their backs.

"Lady Montgomery Baird Watson-Wentworth, surely you should be somewhere else. Perhaps preparing for the New Year?" the chief constable said icily. Arwyn looked suspiciously at the men in the cart as Alex rode around to open the gate at the back of the cart.

"Well, I would be, chief constable, but Mr Hunter and I heard that you were having to spend your New Year's Eve looking for a desperate fugitive, so we thought we would help you so that you could get home," Sarah replied in a sing-song voice that caused the chief constable to grimace slightly.

"And so you have a way of convincing Mr Curran to leave the sanctuary of the church?" Captain Jonnes Smith had clenched teeth as he spoke.

"There's no need. When we went to Chester, these four gentlemen were kind enough to try and prevent us from asking questions about the incident," Sarah began to explain.

"And what would these gentlemen have to do with the incident?" the chief constable asked as he turned to look at the men that Alex was ushering out of the cart.

"These are the gentlemen that Mr Curran apparently assaulted," Sarah replied.

"Apparently?" the chief constable frowned.

"They accused a young girl of stealing from them and tried to take her away. Mr Curran intervened, and these four men attacked him. Mr Lloyd at the Mitre Inn has confirmed the events, and there are five witnesses that can attest to this," Sarah said with a wry smile.

"Which one of you is Charles?" Captain Jonnes Smith roared. The man that remained in the cart froze where he stood.

"I think this one is," Mr Hunter said as he looked at the expression of fear that the man wore.

"McGill, is this the man who reported the crime to you?" the chief constable asked.

"It is, sir," Constable McGill confirmed.

"He has filed a false report. Arrest these men, they can sit in the smallest cell we can find tonight, and I will deal with them tomorrow. If I am feeling merciful, I will not bring my wife with me to show her displeasure at her New Year's Eve being disrupted by their lies," Captain Jonnes Smith announced in a fury.

"So Mr Curran is not to be arrested?" Sarah asked.

"No, he isn't of any interest to me or the police," the chief constable replied gruffly.

"Thank you, chief constable, happy New Year," Sarah said with a slight bow of her head. Captain Jonnes Smith pretended not to hear the pleasantry as he marshalled his men in their duties.

Arwyn cast a glance at Alex as he passed the hunter

and received a slight smile and a nod. When the policemen and their prisoners had left the church grounds, Alex dismissed the cart driver and the lady, and the hunter went into the church to give Mr Curran the good news.

"Ah! Mr Hunter! God certainly does move in the most perfect way, I wanted to talk to you about cricket."

Chapter 19

With Paul Curran free from the threat of arrest, he was able to rejoin the circus before the New Year had arrived.

Sarah and Alex delivered him back to the Bairstow circus with Grace. The lady's maid had opted to remain with the circus overnight to spend time with her sister and attempt to mend some of the fences with her brother.

By the time Mr Hunter and Lady Sarah arrived back at the stables of Grangeback, it was almost midnight.

"Are you coming into the house?" Sarah asked as she rubbed down Black Guy.

"No, not tonight," Alex replied with a thoughtful expression on his face.

"You still haven't forgiven George?" Sarah sighed.

"No, and today has been long enough," Alex leaned over the top of Black Guy's door.

"Then you should go home and rest," Sarah smiled at him.

"Will you come to the circus with me tomorrow?" Alex

asked as he held out a hand towards her.

"You want to be seen together in public?" Sarah teased.

"I do," Alex grinned as Sarah took his offered hand.

"Then how can I refuse?" she asked as she looked at her pocket watch.

"What is it?" Alex asked.

"Happy New Year," Sarah replied as she shut the watch and kissed Alex.

The next morning Alex arrived to take Sarah to the circus. George and most of the household had already left to enjoy the festivities of the circus. Bosworth was the only one remaining in the house as the noise and delights of the circus were certainly not something that appealed to him.

The pair took one of the smaller traps over to the circus, with Harald and Black Guy in the harness. The circus camp had changed overnight. Where before there had only been a series of small tents with fires, carts and carriages between them, there was now a larger canvas tent at the centre of it all.

People streamed into the circus tent. All the gentlemen from the neighbourhood were there – Mr Gregory Kitts, Mr Samuel Jones, Mr Luke Lumb, Mr Timothy Wood, Mr Richard

Ball, Mr Michael Hutton, Mr Joseph Blatherwick, Mr Jake Walker, Mr Stuart Moore, Mr Richard Hales, Mr Gordon Hales and Lord Daniel Cooper were all there. The Egerton family from Tatton Park were all there along with Mr Johnathen Mullaney, Mrs Abigail Mullaney, Reverend Butterfield, and most of Stickleback Hollow, including the butcher, Mr Carter.

Grace wasn't sat in the tent with everyone else, but watched from the flap in the tent where the performers entered and exited.

With so many people in attendance, the circus was filled with gossip and excitement. The sight of Sarah walking arm in arm with Mr Hunter was certainly one talking point amongst the gentlemen of the neighbourhood, but the most interesting news that seemed to be spreading through the crowds at the circus was the announcement of the engagement of Lord Daniel Cooper to Miss Elizabeth Wessex.

It seemed that all people had come to do was to gossip over the events of the last few days as well as the blossoming relationships between the gentry. But when the show began, the audience was held in rapt attention.

The giant Dominic Smith was the circus strongman, who wowed the crowd with feats of strength that seemed impossible to those watching. The small but clever Peter Libby was a master of magic and mysticism, performing tricks that challenged and delighted in equal measure.

The crowd roared with laughter at the antics of the clown Toby Craggs, held their breath whilst Paul Curran threw his knives, and watched in amazement as Emily Read performed gymnastic feats on wires and trapeze.

But the highlight of the circus for all were the lion and the elephant. Matthew Read was the lion tamer, commanding the wild beast to leap through hoops at the crack of a whip. Michael Trott was the elephant handler, commanding the giant, exotic beast to standing on small platforms and spray water at the clown.

The circus was a spectacle, the likes of which had never been seen in Stickleback Hollow before. When the household returned to Grangeback that night, all still eagerly discussing the circus, Bosworth was a little sad he had chosen to miss it.

Grace went to bed happy to have seen her sister, and even happier to have buried at least some of the past with her brother. George was left with the hope that his son would one day forgive him for lying to him for so many years.

For all those at Grangeback, it was a very good start to

the New Year.

Chapter 20

"One has to wonder why it is that I employ you," the cold tone of Lady de Mandeville couldn't even approach the icy look that she fixed Lord Joshua St. Vincent with as he was shown into her study.

"I am very sorry, your grace," Joshua bowed low and tried with hard not to sound insincere.

"You came to me with your pockets turned out, your father had ruined your family with gambling debts and houses of ill repute. You had a pile of bricks that was falling down and not a penny to your name. You begged me to help you for the sake of our friendship as children, and this is how you repay me?" Lady Carol-Ann asked as she rose from the chair she was sat in and walked round to stand in front of the young lord.

"Your grace, it was not as simple as it first seemed. I was surrounded by incompetent people, the best-laid plans can be easily torn apart by the ineptitude of others," Joshua replied.

"Of that, I am all too aware," Lady de Mandeville scowled.

"If you were to give me another chance, I know that I could acquire what you need," Lord St. Vincent promised.

"No, I need you and your brother to go to settle the nerves of some of my agents. The displeasure of the Forbidden City is causing a small amount of resistance amongst some of our contacts. You are to stamp it out," Lady Carol-Ann replied flatly.

"As you wish, your grace. Can I ask, who are you sending to retrieve your property?" Joshua asked.

"I am sending no one," she replied and sauntered towards the fire.

"No one? Then how will you get it back?" Lord St. Vincent followed her to the fire.

"Mr Taylor is already working on that particular problem. I didn't expect either of your schemes to bear much fruit, so I had Mr Taylor assist you as much as he could whilst he devised his own plan to secure my property," Lady de Mandeville said with a half-smile on her face.

"How can he when they know that he works for you?" Joshua asked.

"Harry has always been a very resourceful individual, he knows how to survive, I have no doubt that he will do whatever it takes to fulfil this mission," the duchess replied coolly.

"When do we depart for China?" Joshua asked, changing the subject.

"In the morning. The travel arrangements have all been made, and my attendant has a list of the individuals you need to meet with," Lady de Mandeville replied. She picked a small silver bell up off the mantelpiece and rang it.

The door to the room was opened almost instantly.

"You rang, ma'am?" a young India man dressed in full livery asked.

"Samit, please bring Lord St. Vincent, the instructions and the tickets for his voyage." the duchess said.

"At once ma'am," Samit replied. He wasn't out of the room long, and when he returned, he carried the documents that Lady de Mandeville had asked for on a small silver tray.

"Will that be all, ma'am?" he asked.

"Thank you, yes," the duchess replied. Samit gave a slight bow and shut the doors firmly behind him as he left the room.

He walked down the corridor and then up the stairs to his room in the servants quarters. He didn't have long before he would be needed by the duchess again, but whilst he had a moment, he had a letter to write.

Sarah,

It has been a long time since I last saw you, but we parted as friends. As your friend, I need to warn you, Mr Harry Taylor is in England, and he will do whatever it takes to serve the needs of his employer. He is not the idiot he pretends to be, nor is he by any means harmless or helpless.

Be careful.

Samit

He didn't know whether the letter would arrive in time to warn Sarah of the danger, but he knew that he had to try. Her father had saved his life and paid for him to be educated. He owed a debt of gratitude, he could never repay to the father, but if he could save the life of his daughter, that would be something.

~*~*~

After an attempted kidnapping in Chester, Lady Sarah has a new mystery to solve. With the first kidnapping foiled, the noble woman is certain there will be another, but with so many people in the village for the Grand Tournament, it's easy for kidnappers to go unnoticed. **A Bonfire Surprise in Stickleback Hollow**, Book 5 in the Mysteries of Stickleback Hollow is waiting for you now.

~*~*~

Thank you for reading **The Day the Circus came to Stickleback Hollow**. I hope you enjoyed it! Want to read more about the adventures of Lady Sarah? An exclusive story about them is available for free for all my newsletter subscribers. Visit **https://mailchi.mp/cea2332e3102/cs-woolley-newsletter** to sign up and get access to it, and a whole heap of other exclusive content, offers and contests.

~*~*~

Love the Mysteries of Stickleback Hollow? Then dive into Rising Empire: Part 1, Book 1 in the Chronicles of Celadmore. *Trapped in a political marriage, a queen must fight to save her children, protect both of her kingdoms, and the man she loves, from the forces of darkness.*

~*~*~

Want to help a reader out? Reviews are crucial when it comes to helping readers choose their next book and you can help them by leaving just a few sentences about this book as a review. It doesn't have to be anything fancy, just what you liked about the book and who you think might like to read it.

Use the QR below to leave a review.

If you don't have time to leave a review or don't feel

confident writing one, recommending a book to your family, friends and co-workers can help them choose their next book, so feel free to spread the word.

Historical Note

St. Stephen's Day is what most people would know as Boxing Day. St. Stephen's Day is the Catholic celebration of the first martyr, St. Stephen. It became known as Boxing Day because it was the day that the wealthy would give boxes to their servants that contained what we would consider a Christmas present. The staff were then given the day off. It was also the day that boxes placed in churches on Christmas Day to collect money for the poor were opened and the funds distributed.

The Boxing Day Hunt has been a tradition in Britain for centuries and still exists to the day. Since the ban on fox hunting was introduced in 2004, many hunts have continued to operate scent hunts and drag trails, which are both legal. On Boxing Day in 2016, over 250,000 people came out to follow their local hunts across the UK, which was a record high. Hunts are overseen by the Master of the Hunt who rides at the head of the ride. Dogs are used to follow the scent trails and the riders follow the dogs.

Hunting foxes is not completely outlawed though. Farmers in the UK and Wales are permitted to use up to two dogs to flush out a fox so that it can be shot. In Scotland, an unlimited number of dogs can be used by a farmer to flush out a fox.

Hunting Pink refers to the red jackets that most people think of riders wearing during the hunt. However, hunting pink is not worn by every member of the hunt. Those male riders who are hunt staff and the Master of the Hunt are the ones who will be attired in hunting pink and will have hunt buttons. Hunt buttons are awarded for services in the field and for organising the hunt.

- 4 hunt buttons = Master of the Hunt
- 3 hunt buttons = A hunt subscriber
- 5 hunt buttons = Hunt staff such as huntsmen and whippers-in

Hunt buttons are easy to spot as they are made of brass. The rest of the hunt wear plain black coats. Ladies who are awarded hunt buttons may continue to wear black or navy blue jackets with their buttons and the hunt collar.

In the 1800s, poaching was a problem that plagued quite a few landowners. Two pieces of legislation were passed in relation to poaching in the early 1800s. In 1828 the Night Poaching Act was passed which made it illegal to hunt at night. The second piece of legislation was passed in 1831. This was the Game Act. The Game Act which gave us hunting seasons, rather than people being able to simply hunt anything at any time of year. This also meant that people needed a license in order to hunt game. For those who hunted out of season, they received a fine that was equal to the value of the game they had poached, this restricted hunting for most of the population.

However, this didn't stop poaching. Many poachers were repeat offenders, and some gamekeepers were even assaulted by poaching gangs. When gamekeepers and poaching gangs met, it wasn't a pretty sight. On story that was reported in Huntingdon in 1832 detailed a 30 man strong poaching gang trespassing at 3am and meeting 6 gamekeepers.

"A person who saw the field of action declared if 20 pigs with their throats cut had been left to run about, the ground would not have appeared more saturated with blood. The keepers all of them are dreadfully mutilated, and it is supposed that two of them cannot recover. One of the poachers, named Ball was taken; his head was much lacerated. He had been transported for the same kind of offence before. The route pursued by the poachers might be traced by blood above two miles on the road to Burton Latimer."

The Battle of Waterloo was fought in 1815, and it marked the end of the 20 year long Napoleonic Wars that had ravaged mainland Europe. The battle took place on a muddy field in Belgium and pitted the forces of Sir Arthur Wellesley, Duke of Wellington (also known as the Iron Duke and described by Alfred Lord Tennyson as the last great Englishman), against the Emperor Napoleon.

Though Napoleon had been defeated by the British Fleet under the command of Vice-Admiral Horatio Nelson, 1st Viscount Nelson, 1st Duke of Bronté, KB in 1805 at the Battle of Trafalgar (Nelson died during the battle and has a column in Trafalgar Square in London) he went on a land campaign, conquering European nation after European nation.

The Napoleonic Wars was a very complicated 20 years of military campaigns that involved various coalitions being forged between different European nations to try and defeat Napoleon. This is why the period is described as wars rather than war. To try and explain the entire history that led up to the Battle of Waterloo would take another book. If you want to learn about the Napoleonic Wars, especially the role that the British Army had in the wars, then I highly recommend reading the Sharpe books by Bernard Cornwell.

The first three books are Sharpe's Tiger, Sharpe's Triumph and Sharpe's Fortress are all set in India and will provide you with an idea of the type of actions that Brigadier George Webb-Kneelingroach fought in. Sharpe's Prey (one of my favourite books) deals with the siege of Copenhagen when the British took the Danish fleet to prevent it falling into Napoleon's hands. Sharpe's Trafalgar is the Battle of Trafalgar and Sharpe's Rifles is the first book of the British land campaign against Napoleon. The books go through to the Battle of Waterloo and then to Napoleon's exile on St. Helena in

Sharpe's Devil (the last book in the series). I do have all of them, and no, you can't borrow them.

In short, the Battle of Waterloo was fought on 18th June 1815. Wellington had blocked the road to Brussels and set up a strong defensive position. Wellington was outnumbered, he commanded around 68,000 men as part of an allied force and Napoleon commanded 72,000 men. Wellington had to hold his ground until the Prussian forces, under Blucher, arrived.

Napoleon is reported as saying "He (Wellington) is a bad general and the English are breakfast!" before the battle. The ground was wet from rain, meaning it wasn't easy for Napoleon to manoeuvre. Napoleon began by attacking one of the British defensive positions, Hougoumont farm, and continued to attack it throughout the day. The only French troop to survive entering the farm was an 11-year-old drummer boy.

Wellington is recorded as saying "No troops, but the British could have held Hougoumont and only the best of them at that."

The long and short of it is that the Battle of Waterloo was a long and bloody battle that ended with tens of thousands of men dead and others that were badly wounded and left to die. Blucher and Wellington were victorious, and Napoleon was defeated. Napoleon was sent to St. Helena to live in exile, where he died in 1821. Sir Arthur Wellesley became Prime Minister of Britain in 1828. Though this was not the end of the dramatic life of Sir Arthur, those moments are something that shall be saved for a later book when the Iron Duke makes an appearance.

Swallowtail butterflies are native to India and are absolutely stunning to look at. The lotus is the national flower of India.

Within the landed gentry, younger sons couldn't inherit the family estate, and so the younger sons often took up positions of service to the nation. This came in the form of the clergy, practising law, politics, the medical profession or as officers in the army or navy. Commissions and seats were often purchased for younger sons.

Assam, Darjeeling and Nilgiri tea are all types of Indian tea and are three of my four favourite teas (the fourth is Empress Grey which I have only ever found in Marks and Spencer)

Kleptomania is a psychological disorder that was being observed by French psychiatrists during the 1800s, but it is something that still isn't fully understood. What is known is that kleptomaniacs often have other psychological disorders to contend with such as depression, eating disorders, pyromania and alcohol and substance abuse. It seems to be a disorder that is more common amongst women than men. It is most commonly characterised by the irresistible urge to steal unnecessary items for more than personal or financial gain.

Henry Morton Stanley is the man that is accredited with the phrase "Doctor Livingstone, I presume?" which I borrowed for Mr Claydon's introduction to the series. He was born in 1841, so wasn't actually alive when this book is set, and his meeting with Doctor Livingstone didn't take place until 10th November 1871.

Pocket knives have existed since the Iron Age. The earliest examples were found in Austria and date back to around 600 years before Christ. They became popular and cheap enough for the mass after 1650 when cutlery centres began to produce them. The knife that Mr Claydon is missing would have most likely have been produced in Sheffield, England and would have been a simple peasant knife - the same design as a modern-day Opinel knife.

Attempting to pervert the course of justice is a common-law offence under UK law which means it is a legal precedent that hasn't been legislated but instead has been entirely created by the courts. In simplistic terms, the judgements handed down in court have formed the law rather than an Act being created. I can find no solid evidence of when this term was first used or when the precedent had been set by the courts in order to accurately date attempting to pervert the course of justice.

Sanctuary was abolished for criminal offences in 1623 by King James I, and it was abolished for civil offences in 1697 by William III; however, this didn't mean that it wasn't still provided. In fact, sanctuary can still be claimed in certain churches though there are only very specific situations now when it will be granted.

Slavery was abolished in the British Empire under the Slave Trade Act of 1807, something that was pioneered by William Wilberforce. In 1833 the Slavery Abolition Act was passed, this gave all slaves in the Caribbean their freedom. By 1838 slavery had been fully abolished in Britain and all her territories. Unfortunately, slavery was still conducted throughout the world by other foreign powers which led to persecution of abolitionists and slaves trying to escape to freedom.

The slave trade still exists today in the form of human trafficking (for the sex trade, drugs, black market organs and human sacrifice), debt bondage, decent-based slavery, child slavery, forced and early marriage and forced labour. It is estimated that there are somewhere between 21 million to 46 million people that are currently enslaved in the world today.

The Victorian Circus was something of a spectacle, but there were many different types of them around. They took place under canvas as the idea of the big top didn't exist until the second half of the 19th century. Circus acts included clowns, mystics, knife throwers, acrobats, clowns, elephants, horses

and even aquatic displays.

Touring circuses with large tents existed as far back as 1773, when Philip Astley had a circus that toured to Dublin.

About the Series

Mysteries abound

When her parents die from fever, Lady Sarah Montgomery Baird Watson-Wentworth has to leave India, a land she was born and raised in, and travel to England for the first time. Finding it almost impossible to adjust to London society, Sarah flees to the county of Cheshire and the country estate of Grangeback that borders the village of Stickleback Hollow.

A place filled with oddballs, eccentrics and more suspicious characters than you can shake a stick at, Sarah feels more at home in the sleepy little village than she ever did in the big city, however, even sleepy little villages have mysteries that must be solved.

Set in Victorian England, the Mysteries of Stickleback Hollow follows the crime-solving efforts of Constable Arwyn Evans, Mr Alexander Hunter and Lady Sarah Montgomery Baird Watson-Wentworth.

175

From theft to murder, supernatural occurrences and missing people, Stickleback Hollow is a magical place filled with oddballs, outcasts, rogues, eccentrics and ragamuffins.

Preview from the next book

A Bonfire Surprise in Stickleback Hollow

Mrs Morgan was a woman who was used to charming her clientele and wasted no time in ingratiating herself into Lady Sarah's good graces.

"My lady, how wonderful to see you! How can I assist you today?" Mrs Morgan smiled at Lady Sarah.

"We're here for three gowns for the Grand Tournament ball," Lady Sarah replied as she looked at the reams of material that lined the shelves behind the bespoke counter.

"Three, my lady?" Mrs Morgan sounded surprised.

"Yes, one for myself, one for Miss Read and the other for Miss Roy; all on my account of course," Lady Sarah smiled.

"Excellent, come, ladies, tell me what you have in mind. We'll choose the fabric, the style and I shall take the measurements I need," Mrs Morgan said as he clapped her hands with delight.

Grace and Millie looked at one another with confused expressions on their faces.

"Excuse me, my lady, but neither of us is going to the ball," Grace whispered.

"Of course you are," Sarah replied, "you expect me to go on my own?"

The ladies spent a few hours making all the arrangements for their gowns. Mrs Morgan sent for the cobbler so that he could make shoes to match the gowns for the ladies and the jeweller came to discuss pieces that the ladies might want to wear as well.

Stanley and Lee fell asleep after only an hour of the ladies chatter about what they were going to wear. Miss Roy seemed to be far more knowledgeable than a simple charwoman should have been about fabrics, shoes and jewellery; and she also had a surprising knowledge about the most fashionable styles of gowns in London.

The jeweller had excitedly written down the pieces of jewellery that the ladies wanted, and the cobbler was measuring Lady Sarah's feet when the door to the shop opened, and four men walked in.

It was unusual enough for gentlemen to be in Mrs Morgan's shop, but these four men were as far from gentlemen as you could possibly get.

They were rough-looking men with clothing that reeked of beer and urine. Stanley and Lee were both still asleep, but had they been awake there was very little that they could have done in order to prevent what happened next.

Two of the men seized hold of Millie, and the other two grabbed Grace. The jeweller and Mrs Morgan were all slow to react. Lady Sarah tried to get up to bar the path of the men to the door, but the cobbler was in her way. By the time the lady had managed to push past the cobbler, the two women were already on the street, both screaming for help.

People stared as Lady Sarah rushed into the street, flanked by the two Baker boys. Sarah was fumbling with her purse as she came through the door and eventually pulled out her pistol.

The men were only a few steps away from her; the struggling women were making it difficult for the men to get away quickly.

"Let them go, or I will shoot." Lady Sarah shouted. People were coming out of shops to see what all the screaming was about and the sound of whistles coming closer told the four men that they were running out of time.

Stanley and Lee Baker saw the two men holding Millie

hesitate and rushed at them, shouting. The two boys went for the legs of the men, causing them to trip, freeing Millie. The men fought to try and free themselves, but the Baker boys clung on for dear life.

With Millie free, she scrambled away from the men, and Sarah fired her pistol at one of the men holding Grace. The bullet struck him in the arm, causing him to let go of Grace and cry out in pain.

Sarah began to reload her pistol. Grace was scratching at the man who held her with her free hand. The sound of the policemen approaching grew louder, and the last man standing gave up.

He waited until the police were in sight and pushed Grace into them. People were crowding the street now, and chaos seemed to have erupted as more policemen arrived. The last man slipped away through the crowd as the police handcuffed the other three and took reports of what had happened from the bystanders and Lady Sarah's entourage.

Grace and Millie were taken into Mrs Morgan's shop to recover from the shock. Sarah stood watching the three men being taken away by the police and tried to work out why anyone would want to try and take a charwoman and a lady's maid; and who had known where they were.

Get your copy now!

About the Author

I was born in Macclesfield, Cheshire, UK, and raised in the nearby town of Wilmslow. From an early age I discovered I had a flair and passion for writing.

I began writing at the age of 7 and was first published in 2010. I currently live with my partner, Matt, and our two cats in Christchurch, New Zealand.

As an avid horsewoman and gamer, I also have a passion for singing, dancing, the theatre, and my garden.

Facebook: https://www.facebook.com/AuthorC.S.Woolley

Instagram: https://www.instagram.com/thecswoolley

Website: http://.mightierthanthesworduk.com

For access to exclusive content, contests and freebies, sign up for my newsletter here https://mailchi.mp/cea2332e3102/cs-woolley-newsletter.

Also by the Same Author

The Mysteries of Stickleback Hollow

A Thief in Stickleback Hollow

All Hallows' Eve in Stickleback Hollow

Mr Daniel Cooper of Stickleback Hollow

The Day the Circus came to Stickleback Hollow

A Bonfire Surprise in Stickleback Hollow

Tinker, Tailor, Soldier, Die

What Became of Henry Cartwright

The March of the Berry Pickers

The Advent of Stickleback Hollow

Christmas in Stickleback Hollow

Spring in Stickleback Hollow

Lady de Mandeville in Stickleback Hollow

A Day Trip to Brighton

12 Days of Christmas in Stickleback Hollow

Easter in Stickleback Hollow

Chronicles of Celadmore

Rising Empire: Part 1

Rising Empire: Part 2

Rising Empire: Part 3

Rising Empire Trilogy

Shroud of Darkness

Lady of Fire

End of Days

Shroud of Darkness Trilogy

The Children of Snotingas

WYRD

HILD

The Children of Ribe

FATE

WAR

WIFRITH

DOUBT

SKÅNE

SHIPWRECKED

FEAR

HOME

The Arm Rings of Yngvar Collection

TREASON

MURDER

SEDITION

STRIFE

SUSPICION

ALLEGIANCE

DECEIT

REGICIDE

The Bergkonge Collection

BETRAYAL

Nicolette Mace: The Raven Siren
Medusa
Siren's Call
Shadow
A Shot in the Dark
From Out of the Ashes
The Murder of Michael Hollingsworth
The Case of Mrs Weldon
Hunting the Priest Killer
Beginnings
Manhunt
A Friend in Need
Gangster's Paradise
Ring of Fire
Return of McGregor
Murder in the First
Sabrina
Last Train Home
Til death do us part

How do you solve a problem like Siren?
Siren, Fred and Harry Saga
Filling the Afterlife from the Underworld: Volume 1
Filling the Afterlife from the Underworld: Volume 2
Filling the Afterlife from the Underworld: Volume 3
Filling the Afterlife from the Underworld: Volume 4

Poetry
Standing by the Watchtower: Volume 1
Standing by the Watchtower: Volume 2
Indie Visible: Vol. 1

Shakespeare Simplified
The Merchant of Venice
The Merchant of Venice Key Stage 3 Workbook
The Merchant of Venice Key Stage 3 Teacher's Guide

Further information on these titles can be found at

mightierthantheswords uk.com

Books Adapted by C.S. Woolley for Foxton Books

Level 1 400 Headwords

The Wizard of Oz by L. Frank Baum

The Adventures of Huckleberry Finn by Mark Twain

The Adventure of the Speckled Band by Arthur Conan Doyle

Anne of Green Gables by L. Maud Montgomery

Dracula by Bram Stoker

The Prisoner of Zenda by Anthony Hope

The Lost World by Arthur Conan Doyle

The Little Prince by Antonie de Saint-Exupéry

A Little Princess by Frances Hodges Burnett

The Secret Garden by Frances Hodges Burnett

Level 2 600 Headwords

Moby Dick by Herman Melville

Gulliver's Travels by Jonathan Swift

Alice in Wonderland by Lewis Carroll

Sleepy Hollow by Washington Irving

Treasure Island by Robert Louis Stevenson

Around the World in Eighty Days by Jules Verne

Robinson Crusoe by Daniel Defoe

Beauty and the Beast by Gabrielle-Suzanne Barbot de Villeneuve

Heidi by Johanna Spyri

The Jungle Book by Rudyard Kipling

Level 3 900 Headwords

The Three Musketeers by Alexandre Dumas

Pocahontas by Charles Dudley Warner

Oliver Twist by Charles Dickens

Frankenstein by Mary Shelly

Journey to the Centre of the Earth by Jules Verne

Call of the Wild by Jack London

Level 4 1300 Headwords

The Count of Monte Cristo by Alexandre Dumas

The Merchant of Venice by William Shakespeare

The Railway Children by Edith Nesbit

Jane Eyre by Charlotte Bronte

Level 5 1700 Headwords
The Thirty-Nine Steps by John Buchan

David Copperfield by Charles Dickens

Great Expectations by Charles Dickens

Twenty Thousand Leagues Under the
Sea by Jules Verne

Level 6 2300 Headwords
Kidnapped by Robert Louis Stevenson

The Mysterious Island by Jules Verne

Other
11 Plus Flash Cards

Acknowledgments

Writing can be an extremely lonely profession at times, but thankfully I never have to go through any of the pressures alone. My wonderful Matthew has been a source of constant support to me during all of my writing endeavours since we first met. I couldn't ask for a more fitting partner to share my life or love with.

Writing is not something I stumbled into either, my mother, Helen, took me, and my sisters, to the library every weekend when we were young to get different books, and I always maxed out the number of books I could get. Not only did she encourage me to read, but to write as well. To say I have been writing stories and poetry since I was 7 is not an exaggeration and the development of my writing career is due in no small part to her.

My mother-in-law, Lesley, has also been a source of unflinching and unwavering support, something I could not do without.

To Laura and Sam, who have read and offered opinions, death threats and encouragement on my early drafts, you are true treasures. Amy, you too are worth your weight and more in gold for all your love and support.

It may seem that writers only function alone, but I am blessed to be part of an amazing community of authors whom I know that I have helped push me to even greater heights and success. So to Quinn Ward, Donna Higton, Charlene Perry, Scarlett Braden Moss, Bryan Cohen, Chez Churton, Eliza Green, John Beresford, Rich Cook, Robert Scanlon, Jen Lassalle, Cathy MacRae, Ariella Zoella, and Helen Blenkinsop, my dear friends, thank you.

And finally, to you, dear reader, without you there would be no books, no series, no career. I want to thank you for all the time that you spend reading my work, reviewing it, sharing it with your friends and family. Without you there would be nothing. Thank you from the bottom of my heart. If you haven't already signed up for my newsletter, please do. Newsletter subscribers get access to an exclusive section of my website that is filled with additional content, free stories and

contests that are not available anywhere else. To sign up, just

visit https://mailchi.mp/cea2332e3102/cs-woolley-

newsletter.

Until we meet again in my next book, thank you and adieu.

Made in United States
North Haven, CT
19 April 2022